COUSIN DEAREST

CHRIS BEDELL

BLKDOG

www.blkdogpublishing.com

COUSIN DEAREST

CHAPTER 1

Forget about Grandma being late to her funeral—she wouldn't have shown up. Grandma never arrived on time despite owning several gold watches. And her 60th birthday party this evening under a tent in the backyard of our family's property was no exception. She was nowhere to be seen while I stood by the bar sipping Champagne. But Grandma's tardiness was another reason to love her. She could have been a soap opera actress if she weren't the CEO of a publishing company. Although Grandma's timing wasn't the only reason she could have been a celebrity. She had a constant strut when walking. Like she owned whatever room she occupied.

I lifted my gaze off the Champagne glass, then a scorching sensation jabbed my stomach. A nearby guy's gaze remained fixated on me. Maybe my uneasy stomach should have been upgraded to heart palpitations. Grandma always emphasized how staring was rude. The same kind of behavior often caused an event that would end up on an episode of *Dateline* or give fodder to a future episode of *Law and Order SVU*. But the guy couldn't have been all bad, though. His hot-pink argyle socks would have garnered Grandma's praise. That kind of style took guts.

Fuck it. Starting a conversation was different than giving out personal information. Like that time Grandma answered a crank call, and almost revealed her banking information.

"Can I help you with something?" I asked.

He winked. "Should you be drinking? You don't look twenty-one."

"It's a private party."

My gaze shifted for a beat. The guy held a Champagne flute in his right hand, and I almost sneered. Nothing worse than being hypocritical.

He chuckled. "I was joking."

"Can I get a name?"

"I'm Logan." He offered his hand.

"I'm Casey," I said, giving him a firm handshake with my free hand.

"Nice to meet you."

I gave him a mock frown. "I'm not so sure about that."

Logan rubbed his spiked hair, which was such a light shade of brown that it could have been mistaken for being dishwasher blond. "We're neighbors."

"Excuse me?" I asked.

He took a swig of his drink. "I live in the Cape across the street from you, and have waved at you a few times. I moved to town at the beginning of July."

I bit my lip. Embarrassment wasn't the only reason for my flushed cheeks. The mixture of the carbonation, sweet, and tart flavors of the Champagne jolted my taste buds. My attention soon returned to Logan, though. His collared shirt, blazer, shorts, and white sneakers made him gush worthy. So, having him think I was rude wouldn't help me.

I furrowed my eyebrows. "How did you get invited to

this party?”

"I interned with your grandma over the summer by being one of her slush pile readers. I want to be a writer, and thought the experience would be useful."

"Cool."

"Do you go to Spinderwood High School?" Logan asked.

I nodded. "Yeah. I'm a junior."

His eyes widened. "Same. Maybe I'll see you around sometime."

"I have to know something."

"And what's that?"

"Did you have to be a jerk with your comment?"

Logan shook his head. "I wanted to start a conversation."

"Why me? There are a bunch of other people at the party," I said.

My comment was true. The chattering of voices in the tent meant it was almost at full capacity, because there must have been over one-hundred people. The various Happy Birthday balloons floating inside the tent added to the party atmosphere too. My family was careful when buying the balloons. None of the balloons mentioned Grandma's age. Dwelling on being old would have caused Grandma to go on a melodramatic ramble. Like two weeks ago when I mentioned I was closer to being twenty-one than being ten. My "fact" caused Grandma to bitch about how everyone in her life aged too fast.

"You seemed lonely," Logan said.

"What was interning like?" I asked before finishing my Champagne.

"Interesting. I might have a trilogy worth of material."

I grinned. "I know the feeling."

"The internship wasn't as bad I thought it'd be."

"How so?"

He shrugged. "I thought I'd be worked to death since

I've watched one too many soap operas about companies treating interns badly."

My jaw twitched. "I almost interned with Grandma this summer because I want to be a writer too."

"Why didn't you?"

"I want to make it as a writer on my own merits, and not have people whispering behind my back about me benefiting from nepotism."

He snickered. "Most people would kill to make their dreams come true."

I sighed. "I know. But I can't help being stubborn as shit."

His eyes lit up. "I have a question."

"Sure."

"Is your hair naturally that light?" Logan asked.

Wow. He just had to comment on my hair. I so loved people commenting about my hair color. Listening to babbling about how I should have kept my natural hair color made my day.

"Did I offend you?" he continued.

"It's fine."

Logan was the only one who would get special treatment. Having someone dissect my appearance wasn't ideal. But he asked one question as opposed to hounding me about my appearance 24/7.

His eyes remained fixated on me. "You didn't answer my question."

"No, I'm not a natural platinum blond," I said.

"Cool."

"What made you ask?"

"I was trying to take an interest," Logan said.

"Some people might think bleaching or dyeing hair is silly."

Logan laughed. "Screw them."

"Excuse me?"

He wiggled his eyebrows. "The platinum blond hair looks good on you."

My throat tightened. Making assumptions wasn't ideal because misinterpreting a comment was easy. But I needed to trust my gut. There was something about Logan's comment and constant staring that made me wonder if he was flirting with me.

"I'm trying to flirt with you in case you couldn't tell," Logan said.

"Good to know."

"That's my way of telling you I'm gay," Logan said.

I couldn't help smiling. "I'm bi."

"That's cool."

"Thanks," I said.

He tugged at the sides of his blazer. "What do you like to write?"

"Novels and short stories. What about you?"

"Short stories. I don't have the patience for writing a novel."

I smirked. "It's easier than you think."

A woman in a cocktail dress waved at me. Damn. Mom always interrupted my life when something exciting happened.

"I have to go talk to my mom, but enjoy yourself," I said.

Logan frowned. "Okay."

Analyzing Logan's facial expression would have been appropriate if I had free time, but Mom would wave at me again if I didn't haul ass. Because the writer in me would have dissected whether Logan felt upset about our conversation's abrupt ending.

"Did I do something wrong?" I asked after walking up to Mom.

She clutched her pearl necklace. "Nope. I just want you to fetch your grandmother—she's half an hour late."

"Dad's worried about her?"

"She's his mother," Mom said.

"Fair enough. But where do you think she is?" I asked.

Mom sipped her Cosmo before responding. "She must still be upstairs in her bedroom getting ready."

"Fine. I'll go make sure she's okay."

"Thanks, sweetie. But don't worry. Your date will be here when you get back."

"He's not my date," I said through gritted teeth.

She ruffled my hair. "Whatever you say."

"He just started chatting me up. Although he's gay."

Mom giggled. "That's good. But get going because we don't want your father to have a heart attack."

I rolled my eyes at Mom. She should have known better than to be dramatic. Mom always teased Grandma about how toning down her emotions would have been smart.

I shuffled through the crowd before making my way out of the tent and towards the mansion's front door. My sneakers even crunched against the leaves, which were a mixture of red, orange, and yellow. But it was only the second to last week of August, and pretending summer lasted forever was ideal. Winter followed fall, and I couldn't think about the snow covered front lawn and beach, the ocean being too cold to swim in or being frozen over, or the thick layer of frost coating every window in my family's mansion.

Someone bumped into me as I neared the front door, and I almost cursed.

"Watch where you're going," said the person.

I looked up.

The juxtaposition of the woman's golden-brown highlights against her black hair, which fell a few inches past her shoulders, created a fresh look by combining two colors as opposed to being only one color.

She exhaled a breath. "I'm sorry. I'm having a bad evening."

"No worries."

A gust of wind whistled, but my heart didn't thump louder as I walked away from the woman and approached the front door. Sweat clung to my skin because of how the temperature was still eighty something degrees. So, the breeze didn't have the vindictive biting harshness that winter days had.

I opened the front door and walked by the foyer and towards the staircase.

Ascending the staircase, I stopped at the second floor before I grinned. A rainbow painting of Grandma hung on the wall. Dad had the portrait commissioned several Christmases ago, and I needed a moment to appreciate how unique Grandma was. I couldn't think of anyone else who had a colorful self-portrait. Except maybe the pop art painting of Marilyn Monroe.

Boom. Boom. Boom. The unmistakable sound of gunshots echoed through the house. My pulse vibrated in my ears while I ran. I heard the front door below creak even though I shut it behind me. Yet my back hairs didn't rise. Inventing a problem wouldn't get me anywhere. Checking on Grandma was my biggest priority.

I scurried a few more paces as my shoes squeaked against the wood floor. Maybe, just maybe, the gunshots weren't as dangerous as they seemed. There just had to be an explanation for a gun going off three times in my family's mansion.

I rounded the corner and saw the door to Grandma's room was open. I dashed through and came to an abrupt stop. My hands curled into tight fists while I stomped on the ground the second my eyes drifted down. Grandma lay on the carpet with her white blouse and khaki pants drenched in blood.

My screams echoed through the house. There was no way Grandma could be dead. She was only 60 years old, and still had many years ahead of her.

I kneeled on the ground, then took Grandma's pulse. She didn't have one.

It then occurred to me that I could be in danger. I immediately looked around, breathing a sigh of relief when

I realized I was alone in the room. The killer must have gone down the back staircase. I returned my attention to Grandma, trying to will her to breathe again. This had to be a joke. It couldn't possibly be real.

"What's going on?" asked someone. I jumped at the sound. I hadn't heard anyone coming.

Cocking my head, I turned to see who was there. He was standing in the doorway. "What are you doing here, Logan?"

"I saw you go to into the mansion before hearing the gunshots, and wanted to make sure you were okay."

He walked into Grandma's bedroom and patted my shoulder. "I'm so sorry."

Shaking off the shock, I yelled. "Call an ambulance."

Denial wasn't only something people joked about being a river in Egypt. It was a real coping mechanism. Saying someone shot Grandma didn't quite roll off my tongue.

"Why aren't you calling an ambulance?" I said through my sobs. My throat tightened, with each breath requiring more effort than the previous one. The room also might as well have been spinning despite me not being drunk. Grandma's demise didn't make any sense.

More footsteps echoed, growing louder by the second. Mom, and a few other party guests gasped when their gazes shifted to Grandma after arriving at the bedroom's entrance.

Additional footsteps soon reverberated through the hallway. Dad just arrived.

"Don't look," Mom said, restraining Dad with both arms.

So much for warning Dad. His focus was now on the carpet, and he clapped his hand over his mouth.

I sobbed at everyone. "Grandma is dead."

CHAPTER 2

Grandma's obituary shouldn't have read she died at her 60th birthday party because someone shot her in the chest three times.

But no. Life wasn't some postmodern novel or movie where a character could hit pause and try a different outcome. This was the real world, and my obsession with the German movie *Run, Lola, Run* could wait till later. Although I had to make a confession no matter how awful it was.

I would have chuckled if the murder victim was anyone but Grandma. Not appreciating the twisted irony of someone theatrical going out with a bang was hard. But I kept the depraved thought to myself so nobody would think I was terrible. Besides, I was pretty sure the detective talking to me outside in the hallway by Grandma's bedroom would shout if I didn't answer her question in the next five seconds.

I couldn't pretend my stomach wasn't twisted in ten different directions, though. Something was just claustrophobic about the detective standing in front of me while Mom and Dad were behind me and Logan was to the right of me. I also couldn't forget about sweat oozing out of my pores while the other police officers and crime scene technicians combed through Grandma's room for evidence. But at least I no longer had to stare at Grandma's corpse — she had been put into a body bag and taken away several minutes ago. Her body remaining on her bedroom carpet meant my home would have resembled a haunted house.

My pulse hammered louder in my ears. Having my parents with me was one thing—I was a minor—but I didn't understand why others were still present. Unless the detective planned on also interviewing people in private later to see if there were inconsistencies in what people revealed in public versus what they said one on one.

Dad raised his eyebrows. "The detective asked you a question, Casey."

Mom gripped my shoulder while tilting her head towards Dad. "Relax. His grandma hasn't even been dead an hour yet."

I coughed, clearing my throat. "Like I said, Mom told me to go check up on Grandma. I then heard the gunshots before running into her bedroom."

The detective scribbled something down in her notepad before turning to Logan. "What about you?"

"I wanted to check up on Casey because I saw him going into the mansion right before the gunshots," Logan said.

The detective twirled a strand of hair around her finger after making another note. "Can any of you think of someone who might have had a motive to kill her?"

I shook my head. "Nope."

"No," Mom said.

"No," Dad said.

"Same. I can't imagine anyone who would want to harm Casey's grandma," Logan said.

The detective narrowed her gaze. "And what's your relationship to Rose?"

"I was one of her interns this summer. She's also the one who invited me to the party," Logan said.

The detective cracked a smile. "That was generous of her."

Mom bit her lip. "Is that it with the questions?"

"Yes," said the detective.

"Good," I mumbled.

Dad gave me a dirty look, but I didn't avert my gaze. I could only be polite for so long. Going to bed seemed like the only thing worth doing. So, maybe, just maybe, Grandma would walk into the kitchen tomorrow morning and reveal the whole thing was a joke. I would then find out she had a doppelganger or secret twin sister, and my life would once again be okay. A guy could dream for a second. It wasn't like I would give my family false hope.

"Anyway, I'm sorry for your loss." The detective trekked into Grandma's bedroom, and started talking to one of the crime scene technicians.

Dad frowned at me. "You only have yourself to blame."

"Excuse me?" I asked.

"Not now," Mom said.

"The questions wouldn't have taken so long if you didn't daydream," Dad said.

A lump lingered in my throat. "Please don't take your anger on me because you're upset. That's not fair or right."

Yeah. I refused to waffle about Dad being a jackass. Giving him slack was one thing. But it was another thing for him to take his anger out on me.

Dad grimaced. "My apologies."

Mom tugged Dad's arm. "Come on! We should go downstairs and check on Brad, Rita, Poppy, Tony, and Theresa."

Wait. Time for introductions. Aunt Rita was Dad's

sister, and Brad was her second husband, which made him Poppy's stepdad. Tony and Theresa were my cousins. And Tony and Theresa would have won the prize for saddest teens because of being orphans. Rita, Brad, Poppy, Tony, and Theresa also lived in the mansion with Mom, Dad, and I. Something about Grandma wanting the family to be under one roof.

"I guess," Dad said.

Mom and Dad walked away from Logan and I before descending the staircase. They were soon out of sight.

"Sorry about your Grandma," Logan said.

"Thanks."

"I should go. My mom might be worried about me as a result of the police cars in your driveway."

"No problem."

Logan gazed into my eyes. "Unless you want me to stay?"

Logan sure knew how to tempt me. But no. Chatting could wait till later. Sticking to my plan and going to bed and hoping Grandma would be alive tomorrow morning was my only option.

Holding onto the delusion of Grandma's miraculous resurrection was ultimately nice for one moment. I would have constructed an alternate universe where Grandma was still alive, I reached my publishing dreams by seventeen, and found the love of my life, if wish fulfillment dictated every event in life.

"It's fine. But I appreciate the offer," I said.

"Anytime."

"I wanted to thank you for something else," I blurted.

Logan shook his head. "What?"

"For talking to me tonight."

Logan chuckled. "Not a big deal."

"Being social is hard for me…"

"I don't understand."

My cheeks flushed. Time for a moment of vulnerability, which was great. Nothing like feeling like I was running around town naked.

"Yes. I'm friends with Theresa and Tony. But it's not like I'm Mr. Popular," I said.

Logan smirked. "I'm always here for conversation or whatever."

"Cool. Have a good night."

"You too." Logan tapped my shoulder before lingering for a beat.

Pondering what would happen next would have happened on any other night, but having an empty mind was sometimes okay. And that meant Logan's shoulder tap was just compassion during a difficult time. There was no reason to think about us both staring at each other before getting swept up in the moment and having a spontaneous kiss. Real life would never be able to capture the magic and emotional safety movies offered their characters with a fast-paced romance. Besides, Logan's hand was gone from my shoulder because he just walked away several seconds ago.

A thought soon popped into my head, and I couldn't shake it. The murderer's fast exit prickled my skin. There were two staircases to the second floor, and the murderer must have run to the staircase opposite the one I ascended since I didn't pass the killer. Getting away before being spotted meant the person have been quick on his or her feet, which entailed giving the matter proper planning.

CHAPTER 3

"Hi, guys," I said hours later as I entered the kitchen and didn't bother greeting Uncle Brad, Aunt Rita, and Poppy with a smile.

Going to bed was an exercise in futility since I wouldn't get a good night sleep. Grandma hadn't even been dead for twelve hours. And I might as well have not been alone if I was just going to stare at my bedroom ceiling for the next six or seven hours. Because Grandma's silly expression about misery loving company was right.

"Hi, Casey." Poppy pushed a lock of her blonde hair out of the way.

"Good to know I'm not the only one who can't sleep." I walked over to one of the kitchen cabinets and grabbed a snack from a tin. Then, I nibbled on the sugar cookie.

"Your parents, Theresa, and Tony crashed a little while ago." Aunt Rita said, grabbing a tissue from the box on the kitchen counter. She rubbed her eyes before blowing her nose and tossing it into the trashcan.

Poppy's jaw trembled. "I can't imagine how you feel, Casey. You were the closest to Grandma."

"I don't understand who would do this," I said, shaking my head.

"Twisted is twisted. There's no use in reasoning with a murderer," Poppy said.

"It's so wrong." Aunt Rita grabbed another tissue and wiped the new tears away. But she didn't throw out the tissue. Instead, she squeezed the tissue. "I just hope the police catch her killer.

"The police might never catch Grandma's killer," Poppy said.

Aunt Rita dropped her tissue. "Why would say that?"

No offense to Aunt Rita, but she should have known better to ask that question. Poppy always said the wrong thing. However, Poppy wasn't all terrible. She donated half of the money she received from her sweet sixteen party to an environmental charity.

"I'm trying to be realistic," Poppy said. "Honoring Grandma's legacy matters most."

"You two were the ones that were hard to find," Aunt Rita said.

Poppy rolled her eyes. "Brad took me back to my room so I wouldn't make a fool of myself while being tipsy."

"Then how come Casey discovered Grandma first?" Aunt Rita asked. "Also, you really should know better about not getting trashed at public events."

Poppy picked her nail. "I needed to cool off for a moment and not do anything dumb. You should be proud of me for recognizing a potential problem before it happened."

"Whatever," Aunt Rita said.

Uncle Brad glared at Poppy, but she rolled her eyes. Aunt Rita then clenched her jaw while remaining silent. And I didn't even blame anyone for not saying another word. Only so much could be said about Grandma's murder in one night. Because I didn't need an incentive for not making a snide comment. Silence was sometimes best—some situations were simply beyond words.

CHAPTER 4

Sunlight snuck through my bedroom curtains a few hours later. I put my exercise T-shirt and shorts on before sliding a sock onto each foot and slipping into my sneakers. Staying in bed might have been tempting. Yet I wouldn't wallow in misery all day. Life might have been bleak, but I could exercise.

Going for walks was also an easy way stay healthy. There was no doubt Grandma would have lectured me about how it was never too early to fend off death. Grandma was the one who took all those daily supplements, after all.

"Hi," Logan said several minutes later after I stepped foot onto the street.

He held a newspaper in one hand while he stood a few feet away from me at the end of his driveway. Interesting. Reading a newspaper was something I should have deduced from our first interaction. Writers were probably one the few types of people who appreciated having a physical copy of the newspaper. They understood the importance of seeing their work in print.

"Morning." I walked over to him.

"I don't suppose you got any sleep?" he asked.

"No."

Logan's lips quivered. "Plans for today?"

"I was gonna go for walk," I said.

"That's cool. Are you the first one up?"

I snickered. "Yes."

"Good to know you're still capable of laughing."

A bird chirped before landing on Logan's front yard, and lowered its head and nibbled on something. It then clapped its wings together before flying away.

Damn. If only I was a bird—life would have been simpler. I wouldn't have had to complicate what living the rest of my life without my grandmother entailed. Instead, I would've only been worried about survival.

"Would you wanna hang out sometime?" Logan asked.

"Sure. Why don't we exchange cellphone numbers?"

We handed our iPhones to each other before giving them back a moment later. Glee even radiated from my grin for one fleeting moment. Something went my way, and I couldn't help appreciating said fact. Needing a win made me human.

Logan leaned forward. "Don't be a stranger."

"I won't."

"Good. Because I'm selective about giving out my number."

"Really?" I asked, almost laughing.

"Yup. And you don't have to worry about bothering me. I'm happy to give you a distraction if you need one."

Life was a lot of things. But even I appreciated the universe's awkward timing. Hanging out and getting to know Logan was now at the top of my priority list since I didn't have to choose between my grief and wanting to know Logan more. The Logan situation also meant adding excitement to my life. Getting to know someone new was one of the few times when a little mystery was okay.

CHAPTER 5

"I'm glad you accepted my offer," Logan said several days later.

We sat inside at Mona's Madness, which was a frozen yogurt shop in town on Main Street. Being indoors instead of outside wasn't silly despite not a cloud in the sky. The temperature was once again back up in the eighties, meaning copious amounts of sweat, which was the last thing my date needed to see. I also had no qualms about taking advantage of free air conditioning.

Wait. I referred to Logan as my date even though we hadn't defined if today was a hangout or date. Whatever. Worrying about whether to DTR or not could wait. I sometimes understood the importance of living in the moment when it came to hanging out with a possible future boyfriend.

"Me too. Besides, it's the perfect day for this outing." I took another spoonful of my frozen yogurt before the vanilla flavor electrified my taste buds.

"Agreed. Although it's my first time coming here."

Logan took a bite of his frozen yogurt.

He got chocolate yogurt. But I wouldn't chastise him for liking chocolate even though I preferred vanilla. Having everything in common with a friend or potential boyfriend would have been boring. Besides, Grandma always emphasized liking the main characters not knowing everything about their respective love interests in the romance novels her company published.

I winked. "I'll give you a break because you're new to town."

"Thanks."

"You were also right about needing to get out of the house," I said.

"Do you know when the funeral will be?"

"Saturday," I murmured.

"I hope it's okay, but I'd like to go." Logan shoved another bit of frozen yogurt into his mouth.

Wow. He was almost done with his frozen yogurt while I wasn't even halfway through mine. It wasn't like we got different sizes; we hadn't. But too bad there wasn't a prize around for fastest frozen yogurt eater. I would have gushed and campaigned for Logan to win the award if such a thing existed.

I nodded. "Sure."

"I didn't know her that long, but she was a friend to me."

"What do you mean?"

His cheeks turned bright red. "There was one stressful day at the office and she took me out clubbing after work."

I wrinkled my nose. "Yet you gave me grief at the party."

"It wasn't anything foolish. We just had two martinis each," Logan revealed.

"Were your parents suspicious?" I asked.

He laughed. "Nope. We got coffee afterwards to kill time."

I rolled my eyes. "They really served you?"

"She bribed the bouncer and bartender," Logan said.

I burst into laughter—Logan provided me with a bigger gift than he realized. Having another story of Grandma was a good thing. This conversation gave me an opportunity to learn something new about her, and I'd take said chance. Almost as if discussing something new about Grandma meant she wasn't dead. Not completely, at least.

"Where is the funeral going to be?" Logan continued.

"In town at the St. Thomas church."

The door placard chimed while a woman with salt and pepper colored hair walked into the frozen yogurt shop. But I should have been more concerned about her white colored blouse. And I wasn't trying to be a pervert, as the lady shuffled towards the counter while Logan and I remained seated at a table in back. I couldn't help thinking about another anecdote from Grandma's past. Grandma once sported a white long-sleeved blouse at her birthday party two years ago like the woman that entered the shop moments earlier. And Grandma couldn't shut up about how fashionable she thought the shirt was because everyone kept staring at her. Yet they weren't admiring her. At least for the reasons she thought they were. Grandma had been oblivious to the restaurant's bright lighting in the room, which meant her blouse was see through. Although I had never been more thankful for a bra in my life. Being scarred at fifteen wasn't on my bucket list.

"How's your family doing?" Logan asked.

"I'd rather talk about something else," I said.

Yup. Now wasn't the time to mince worries. If Logan and I were gonna build any kind of connection—whether platonic or romantic—then we needed to at least be a little bit honest with each other. Life was already complicated enough without putting on a mask for another person.

He grinned. "Sure. No worries."

"Have you written anything new?"

"Yes. But I'm still editing it." He paused for a beat.

"I'm just thankful I found time to write this summer despite my internship."

I ate another scoop of my frozen yogurt. "That's good. Although I'd be worried about burning out."

"What about you?"

"I finished editing a story a week ago, but I've been too afraid to share it with anyone."

His pupils dilated. "I'm sure it's great. I'd love to read it sometime."

"Thanks. Although I might sit on it for another month or two."

Logan pointed to the right side of my cheek. "You have some frozen yogurt there."

It would have been silly getting angry at Logan because he hadn't screamed it for the cashier and couple of other customers to hear. There was also a difference between helping people and criticizing them.

"Is it gone?" I asked, after wiping my face.

Logan laughed again. "You made it worse. Here, I'll get it."

He slid his elbows onto the table while he leaned a little closer.

Logan touched my lip, creating brief static while he wiped the frozen yogurt off my face. We even looked each other in the eye. But we didn't kiss. Spoiling my dynamic with Logan by being too forward might ruin things.

He rested a hand under his chin. "Wanna tell me the plot of your new story?"

Discussing their work might have made some writers nervous, but talking about my writing was welcomed with open arms. Dwelling on something other than wondering if Logan and I had chemistry ensured I wouldn't make a fool of myself.

"Sure. I'd be happy to," I said.

CHAPTER 6

Someone knocked on my bedroom door hours later while I laid on my bed reading a book.

"Come in," I said.

The door opened, revealing my twin cousins Tony and Theresa. They were the same age as me in addition to being juniors and attending the same high school. Although that was where the similarities stopped. I was a writer while Tony was on debate team and Theresa was into fashion. They also happened to be redheads where I was had light brown hair that was bleached blond.

I put my bookmark back in the book and closed it before putting the novel aside. "What's up?"

"Not much." Theresa replied "Your mom just wanted to know if you want anything special for dinner."

Theresa and Tony walked over to my bed and sat down next to me.

"Pizza would be nice," I said.

Tony rubbed his hands together. "Sounds good."

Theresa sighed. "We also wanted to check up on

you."

"Excuse me?" I asked.

"We know you were the closest to Grandma," she said.

Perhaps Theresa and Tony had more in common with Poppy than I realized if they were privy to Grandma having the closest relationship with me. But I didn't know whether to scream or smile. There was a thin line between being considerate and hovering too much. I wasn't glass, and wouldn't shatter into a bunch of shards.

I bit my lip. "I'm taking it one day at a time."

Yup. Cheesy sayings contained a hint of truth. Trying not to get ahead of myself was my only option. I didn't need to know how the rest of my life would turn out okay. Trusting life would be fine was enough. Besides, I wasn't hiding my emotions from myself. I screamed into my pillow and punched it several times since Grandma died.

"That's a good plan." Theresa brushed a piece of lint off her dress.

Yeah. She had a strapless cocktail dress on even though we weren't going anywhere tonight. Fashion was her primary interest, and she happened to be wearing a Theresa Gilbert original dress. Grandma would have praised Theresa if she were here. Theresa was her own best advertiser. Nobody could advocate for herself better.

"This must be hard for you guys because of what happened to your parents," I said.

Tony gritted his teeth. "Yes. But there are a lot of positive memories to focus on."

"I hope the police will catch her killer," I said.

"The murderer is usually someone the victim knows," Tony replied.

Theresa nudged Tony's shoulder.

Tony glared at his sister. "I can't help if that fact is true."

Please. As if I needed another reason for an increased heartbeat. Musing about how the murderer could have been someone close to Grandma would only guarantee more sleepless nights. That fact meant I might have known the murderer, which only added to my stress. I wanted nothing more than to worry about discovering who killed Grandma before she was even in the ground.

CHAPTER 7

Grandma would have been proud if she saw there wasn't one empty seat in the whole church at her funeral. And I wasn't being morbid by taking pleasure in her death. I needed to think about anything besides how today was the day my family would put Grandma to rest.

My family occupied the first row on the right, and I happened to be seated on the aisle seat. An increased heartbeat due to my claustrophobia wasn't worth it today. My life already seemed like I was stuck in a box as a result of Grandma's death, and I didn't need to be "trapped" by being crushed between two people.

Crushed was a harsh word to use, yet I won't budge. I deserved any comfort within reason. It wasn't like I wanted to jump off a roof because I thought I was superman.

Theresa leaned into my ear. "Are you okay?"

I nodded. "Yes."

"Quiet," Tony whispered. "The service is about to start."

Giving Tony grief for being blunt might have happened on any other day, but there was no good reason to start trouble. The priest now hovered in front of the podium while going over his speech.

I couldn't help snickering a bit. One glance at my watch revealed it was 9:55 A.M., which meant the service would start a couple of minutes early. The official timing in the program mentioned it was supposed to start at 10:00 A.M. Yet the priest just did the testing-1-2-3 bit, which meant starting the service was the only thing left to do. Although I should have explained my minor amusement. Grandma arrived late to every event in her life, but her funeral was ahead of schedule.

"I've directed a lot of services, but it never gets easier," said Father James. "I'm always reminded of how precious life is because the old cliché about people not knowing how much time they have on Earth is true."

Great. Father James used the word cliché in his speech. Including that word really inspired confidence. His first impression with his wrinkled pages for his speech wasn't reassuring enough, and he sealed the deal with being Mr. Old Fashioned.

Logan must have appreciated the details too. He followed through with his promise and sat two rows behind me.

Father James sipped water from his bottle before continuing. "The important thing is not to despair. Sure. Some of you must be thinking that's cheesy to mention at a funeral, but my point is true. Death doesn't have to erase someone from existence. We can all honor people who are dead. Like planting a tree in the person's honor or eating their favorite food."

Father James meant well, but I naturally fidgeted despite having an aisle seat. I just had to notice the stained-glass window behind Father James showing a dove flying towards a woman. The etching was actually quite remarkable. It had a mix of red, orange, yellow, green, blue, and purple.

Sure. Some people might have thought rainbow colors were corny, but not me. Having a unique image be present at Grandma's funeral further honored her. She would have enjoyed the stained-glass window artwork because of the rainbow painting of her on display at the mansion.

"We can also take comfort with how our loved ones are never truly gone because they are always watching over us from Heaven."

Wow. Father James was still speaking. Hopefully, nobody would give a quiz about his eulogy. I wouldn't have just failed it. I would have gotten a goose egg since Father James was lucky if I picked up on every fifth sentence.

Enough critical ramblings, though. Father James was right. I could honor Grandma despite her being dead. I owed her for so much. And I wasn't talking about how she let the whole family live in her mansion. I was referring to how she gave me the confidence to be my true self without any equivocation or hesitation. Big moments aren't the only events that shape our lives. Quiet moments impact people too.

***

Sunlight radiated from the sky a day three years earlier, and onto my family's beach, which was beyond the front yard. I happened to be lying down on a beach towel while salt water wafted through the air as I read a book. And I would have thought nothing could go wrong now, but then someone screamed.

I lifted my gaze off the book. Grandma stood a few feet away from me at the bottom of the steps. Although there was no need to be dramatic about the steps. There were only three of them, connecting the grass to the beach.

I furrowed an eyebrow. "Everything okay?"

"Just out of breath. That's all."

"Do you want me to go back inside and get you a glass of water?"

She shook her head. "That's okay. I was just worried about making it across the property without tripping."

I remained silent.

"Besides, I don't think you would be too comfortable inside," Grandma continued.

"What makes you say that?"

"You left the kitchen to read a book on the beach."

"I wanted to enjoy the nice day."

Grandma giggled. "It's just us, Casey."

"What are you getting at?"

She walked over to me before sitting down on the sand. "Do I have to spell it out?"

I hung my head lower. "Yes."

"I know Uncle Brad made you uncomfortable when he asked if you had any boyfriends or girlfriends."

"No offense, but you're reading into things too much," I said through gritted teeth.

She glared at me. "Even I'm not that dense."

I sighed. "So?"

"Don't let anyone put you in a corner. Be proud of who you are," Grandma said.

Interesting. She put my mind at ease without being too awkward, which meant giving her an A for effort. Someone people might not have been as lucky as me with having such a cool Grandma.

"Is my sexuality that obvious?" I asked.

Asking my question wasn't about being redundant. Knowing how other people viewed me compared to how I viewed myself created intrigue. There was a good chance that there was a difference between how I perceived myself and how others perceived me.

"Yes. But it'll only be a big deal if you make it one. I also want you to know that Uncle Brad means well. He wasn't trying to upset you. He just isn't always the most graceful person."

"I can't help it if I think both Scarlett Johansson and Robert Pattinson are hot."

"I know, I know."

***

Someone started plucking a harp, ending my digression.

Okay. Father James must have finished his speech since everyone has started flocking towards the lobby. But I wasn't kidding about flunking a quiz if someone picked my brain about Father James's eulogy. Because I didn't need to add being fucked seven ways to Sunday at the top of my bucket list. No thanks. Grandma's murder was enough darkness to last several lifetimes.

Tony gazed at me. "Gonna get up?"

"No. I just wanna be by myself for a minute."

"Sure," Tony said.

Theresa patted my shoulder before her and Tony shuffled out of the row and towards the lobby.

"It was a great service, Casey," Logan said.

"Thanks."

Logan got up from his seat a few rows down from me before sitting down in aisle seat right behind me.

His eyes widened. "I couldn't help noticing you were distracted."

I remained silent while breaking my eye contact with Logan. I just didn't know how to feel about Logan addressing my current emotional state. On the hand, Logan's comment revealed he was considerate. Yet I didn't wanna scare him away by seeming like too much of a wreck because of Grandma's death. Even nice people had their limit for what they tolerated.

I sucked on my teeth. "You caught me."

"Didn't mean anything bad by it."

"No worries."

He coughed into his right blazer sleeve. "I remember

when I lost my grandfather."

"Sorry to hear that."

"Thanks. Although it was seven years ago. But that isn't my point. My point is, it gets better."

A lesser person would have criticized Logan for implying life would get better. But I didn't have the energy to argue with anyone. He also hadn't said anything bad. The point was, he wanted to comfort me. And I took it. I could at least pretend to appreciate the importance of taking moments at face-value despite never being capable of following that advice.

"I'm sorry. I know I'm bombing," Logan stammered.

"Don't worry about it."

"I want you to know I'm here for you. Even if all you need is a moment of serendipity such as going to the movies," he said.

I chuckled. "I'll keep that in mind. Although I don't think any theatre is playing my favorite movie."

"And what's that?"

"*Run, Lola, Run*," I said.

He gave me a mock frown. "That's your favorite movie?"

"Have a problem with that movie?"

"Yeah. It's really pretentious."

No offense to Logan, but he was on dangerous ground. How anyone could criticize *Run, Lola, Run* was beyond me. Not when there were dozens of worse movies.

"I'm kidding," Logan continued. "I've never seen the movie. Although I have heard of it, and would be happy to watch it with you."

Good save, Logan. So, I was more impressed with Logan than I realized. Most people might not have pivoted the conversation like he just had.

Someone grunted, and I cocked my head. A woman seated a few rows behind Logan was sobbing louder than a stomping rhino. She zipped open her purse and pulled out a tissue and blew her nose. She then got up before pushing a lock of hair out of the way.

Wait. I had seen the woman before. She was the same disgruntled woman from Grandma's birthday party.

Her high heels soon scraped the ground, and she disappeared into the mob of people in the lobby.

I looked back at Logan. "I'd be happy to watch *Run, Lola, Run* with you. I actually own the DVD."

"No surprise there," Logan said.

I glance forward for a beat. A ring was on the floor near the woman's seat. The ring even sparkled from the sunlight glinted against it.

Worrying about the ring was pointless, though. Intellectualizing how empathy was important didn't mean it was my job to solve every problem in the world. It didn't. The empty feeling inside me from Grandma's death was obstacle enough—I was just gonna have to find a way to live with my grief.

CHAPTER 8

I entered Grandma's study a couple of hours later even though Grandma might have criticized me for being rude. The wake was still going on in the kitchen and the living room at my family's mansion. And I was pretty sure that Mom and Dad would have also disapproved. Like that time when I was seven and excused myself from dinner without asking my parents if I could go to my bedroom and watch television.

But fuck it. I needed to take a moment for myself because I couldn't always live to please other people.

Yes. Grandma would never be in her study again. But if sitting down at her desk in her wheelie chair allowed me to be close to her, then good.

The walls might have been the same shade of violet they had always been, but the study needed to be cleaned. Thick clumps of dust coated the desk, and I was sure in a matter of seconds, I would cough up a lung. I then would have had to explain to Mom and Dad about why I only had one lung. And I so wanted to do that. Nothing more fun than digging my own grave.

Grandma's desk wasn't all terrible despite the dust and stacks of folders, though. She had the snow globe of the Eiffel Tower on her desk after all this time. Yet I should have been more interested in the folded-up piece of paper resting under the snow globe.

Picking up the snow globe and putting it aside was only natural. I had to read the note even if there was a good chance of it being mundane.

As I read it, my heart thumped faster. Apparently, Grandma had given up a child for adoption when she was a teen. That child, now a woman, had reached out to her. The letter was dated only a couple of years ago, as opposed to be some old obscure document.

Wow. People learned new things every day even when school wasn't in session. Because I would have never guessed someone as prim and proper as Grandma would have had a secret child. Although Grandma was capable of surprises. Like with her living and dying for coupons. Call me crazy. I just didn't understand why a well-off person believe coupons were a lifesaver.

Fuck. Footsteps echoed, which meant someone could be coming to fetch me. Whatever. I stuffed the letter into my blazer pocket. And I would avoid thinking about the revelation. Grandma deserved to be honored in the present and her past could wait till later. Not even I would deface a dead woman's legacy by being obtuse.

CHAPTER 9

I walked into the kitchen several mornings later and found Dad by the stove. The teapot rested on the front right burner. A red light illuminated the corresponding button, meaning it was on. A mug was on the counter next to the stove with a teabag inside it. Seeing the mug he selected caused me to suck in a breath. Sure. Dad hadn't done anything bad, but grief wouldn't disappear after the funeral.

Nostalgia soon filled my insides. The mug Dad selected was Grandma's favorite mug, and had the image of several leprechauns etched on it. I even almost mentioned how Grandma sometimes spiked her coffee with booze when the universe fucked with her if I felt like being cute. Like that time when the printer made a mistake on a print run of ten thousand books, and she threw a tantrum because they almost charged for the correction.

"Morning," Dad said.

"How did you sleep?" I asked

He shrugged. "Okay considering everything that

happened."

I rolled my eyes. Dad was dressed in a blazer, buttoned-shirt, khaki pants, argyle socks, and black designer dress shoes. His briefcase also rested on the kitchen counter next to his mug. And I couldn't forget about his combed back. There was a difference between being diligent and lazy, though. Nobody would have judged him for needing a few more personal days. It wasn't like he would win some sort of award for being the first person to arrive back to work. Besides, Grandma always took off as much of August off as possible. Something about living life to the fullest.

"Don't tell me you're returning to work?" I asked.

"I don't have a choice."

"I thought the company was taking time off?"

"I need to go over contracts," Dad said.

Yup. My ears hadn't deceived me. Dad worked with Grandma and Uncle Brad at the publishing company. But his job wasn't exciting like Grandma's publisher duties. Dad was one of the company's head lawyers.

"There's something I have to talk to you about," I blurted.

I chose not to bring up the letter when I was supposed to have been engrossed in conversation at the wake. If I had, I would have needed to pray Dad's reaction to my discovery wouldn't have been worse than someone quizzing me on Grandma's eulogy. Flunking an imaginary quiz was one thing, but I didn't need to stutter because of Dad's wrath.

His eyes lit up. "And what's that?"

"I found a letter in Grandma's study."

The teakettle whistled, and steam oozed out of the spout. Dad let the teakettle rattle for a few moments before flicking the switch. He poured the water into the mug before returning the teakettle to the stove. He gave the teabag several dunks into the mug and threw it out in the garbage can residing in the pantry door below the stove. I nearly teased him about taking so long with making his tea. Almost like how Grandma used to wake up at quarter to six every morning and spent an hour fussing over her hair and makeup after getting dressed and showering. But even I was capable of picking my battles—I valued my life and didn't need Dad's vengeance.

His lips curled. "What kind of letter?"

I exhaled a long breath. "There's no easy way for me to say this. But did you know Grandma had a baby as a teenager and gave her up for adoption?"

Dad didn't flinch. "Yes. I knew."

I let the shock of dad's knowledge and the fact he and grandma had kept it hidden from me slide. I swallowed as I composed myself.

"Did you ever meet her?"

"No." He picked up his mug and blew on it before taking a small sip.

I raised an eyebrow. "Did Grandma ever meet her?"

"I don't know."

Dad gripped his tie, which had the image of Mickey Mouse on it. "I wouldn't dwell on the letter."

Perhaps Dad was more on edge than I realized if he needed to grip his tie for a distraction. But he hadn't yelled or lectured me, which was something to be glad about. I hadn't gotten random amnesia and was very much aware of his flared nostrils during the police question the night of Grandma's murder.

"Who is that guy you talked to at the funeral?" he asked.

Great. Dad noticed how I got sidetracked during the funeral since I stayed behind and continued sitting when everyone else chatted in the lobby. And it wasn't like I could stomp my feet and scream. Because my current situation's twisted irony didn't escape me. Having Dad inquire about my love life was an example of life returning to some sense of normalcy. That was the type of thing a teen could expect from their parent.

I scratched my forehead. "I wish the police would get a lead."

Perfect. I saved myself any possible embarrassment by changing the subject. But fair's fair. He changed it first. The CIA could have recruited me if writing wasn't my first passion. Thinking on my feet proved I would make a good spy.

"This isn't a TV show where police wrap up a murder in 42 or 43 minutes," Dad snapped, then took a deep breath. "I'm sorry. I shouldn't have raised my voice. I'm just still adjusting."

"No problem."

"You didn't answer my question," Dad blurted.

Shit. Dad wasn't clueless and just had to notice my evasiveness. So much for adding being a CIA agent to my list of possible careers.

"His name is Logan. He's our neighbor," I said.

Dad had more tea before speaking. "I met him and his mom when they first moved in."

"He's just an acquaintance."

"Really?"

I laughed. "Please don't embarrass me."

"It'd be good to have another friend," he said.

I scowled. "Meaning?"

"Nothing. It's just your only young once and should have a little fun. You only hung out with Tony and Theresa this summer."

"That wasn't my fault. Sadie was at that summer painting residency."

Yeah. Summer almost made me pull out my hair regardless of Grandma's death. Not dwelling on Sadie's absence was a careful calculation. Thinking about not spending the summer with my best friend would have only caused more loneliness for me.

"When does Sadie come back again?" Dad asked.

"In three days."

"Fantastic."

"I wish I knew who hated Grandma enough to kill her," I said.

He remained silent.

"What?" I continued. "You don't think I'm foolish for wondering who killed Grandma?"

"I didn't say that."

"Then what's your point?"

His jaw trembled. "You need to trust everything will work out."

"How can you be so optimistic?"

"It's my only option." Dad chugged the rest of his tea, and grabbed his briefcase. "Anyway, I hope you have a good day."

His shoes squeaked against the floor and he was gone before I blinked. Dad hadn't said something damning, but I should have given him a little sass. Not thinking about Grandma's murder was impossible. Wanting closure only made me human.

Also, I wasn't being presumptuous by believing her death was murder. The conclusion was obvious from the second I spotted Grandma's corpse. One of the detectives working the case stopped by and gave us the official word how the medical examiner ruled Grandma's death a homicide. No offense to the detective, but the revelation hadn't changed my life. My family and I deduced for ourselves murder was the reason Grandma died. It wasn't like she had an allergic reaction to a wasp.

Something beeped.

I pulled my iPhone out of my pocket, discovering I had a new text from Logan: *Doing anything fun today?*

Not really. What about you? I typed.

My iPhone buzzed again: *Nope, I'm not. Any interest in hanging out?*

Contemplating my response had nothing to do with writing the next great American novel. Seeming desperate was still foolish. But perhaps I read into things too much. I needed to enjoy every possible fleeting moment of happiness. No telling when the next bad thing would happen.

Sure, I typed back.

My iPhone pinged. Wow. Maybe Logan would win the award for fastest responder of the year.

My eyes returned to the phone's screen: *Any ideas about what you want to do?*

You could come over to my house and we could watch Run, Lola, Run, I texted back.

My eyes shifted back to my iPhone in a matter of seconds: *Perfect. How about I come over in two hours?*

Sounds good, I typed back.

CHAPTER 10

Someone knocked on my bedroom door a couple of hours later after I put the DVD into my laptop, which was on my bed. I only needed one guess to know who stood on the other end of the door. My heart had been fluttering for the last fifteen minutes. There was nothing like spending time with my crush/future boyfriend to impact me more than tapping my feet from drinking too much coffee. Grandma would have sympathized with me if she were here. She once told me about how arriving at a date two hours early when was a teen. Something about needing time to pull herself together.

"Come in," I said before getting off my bed and standing.

Logan entered my bedroom while holding two venti Starbucks coffee cups.

He smiled. "Hi."

My eyebrows arched. "You went to Starbucks?"

"It was the least I could do since you're supplying the location. I remembered you said you like Caramel Macchiatos."

Getting my favorite Starbucks beverage was one surprise I didn't mind. Whether people realized the truth or not, both little and big actions defined character. Logan doing something considerate revealed he was once again a considerate person. And I valued said fact more than they he realized. Nothing wrong with some making an effort even if always expecting people to read minds was naïve. Logan did something without having to be asked, which was more than some teenagers might have been able to say about their potential future boyfriend or girlfriend.

"How much do I owe you?" I asked.

"Don't worry about it."

"Really?"

He laughed. "I won't go bankrupt from an impromptu Starbucks trp."

"Cool. But I have to ask. What did you get for yourself?"

"A Toffee Nut Latte."

"I had it once. Although it's nice as good as a Caramel Macchiato."

No debate necessary about a Caramel Macchiato versus a Toffee Nut Latte. There was nothing like the explosion of the mixture of the caramel and bitter espresso jolting my taste buds. However, the last drop was the best. Baristas didn't just top a Caramel Macchiato with caramel. They also squirted a few pumps of caramel before pouring in the milk and espresso shots. I ate, breathed, and lived Starbucks. In fact, I was pretty sure the *Guiness Book of World Records* should have contacted me for the record on who could visit Starbucks the most times in a month.

"We can put the beverages down on the bed board," I said, pointing.

"Sure." Logan put the two cups where I told him to place them.

A silence ensued for a beat after I made myself comfortable by lying on my stomach with my feet in the air as my head was only a couple of inches from my laptop. But Logan continued standing right next to me. And I kind of wanted to say something. Yet my heart hadn't stopped beating faster since Logan's arrival.

Fuck it. Logan was worth being anxious for, and there was nothing wrong with making the situation easier by letting him sit on my bed. Grandma would have even been proud of me if she were here. Something about how taking imitative showed the type of person someone really was.

I snickered. "There's plenty of room for two. I promise I don't bite."

"Cool."

I scooted to the right, making room for Logan. He took my cue and was now on his stomach with his feet in the air. And that was fine. We already hung out a few times and were only watching a movie. Letting him on bed wouldn't make me lose all my clothes. I was only being a good host. Although Logan's respect was worth smiling about regardless of how we would have been carefree in a perfect world. Some people might not have waited for my invitation to lie down on my bed. And Logan now had another check in the plus column. But I couldn't get ahead of myself. Seeing a movie at home wasn't the same as getting spruced up for a fancy date. Yet hanging out with him still felt like I date. Grandma used to mention how people didn't always need labels to tell them something was true. Like when Grandma would sometimes have a day from hell and swore the universe was out to get her.

I chuckled louder this time. "I hope you like the movie."

"I'm sure it'll be great."

Awesome. Another check in the plus column. His positive attitude about the movie was a reason for my pulse to increase even more. It wasn't like Logan plotted against me and was only being nice as a cover. Nope. Something like that would have only happened in the movies, television, and when I reflected about Grandma's life.

"Enjoy," I said before hitting the spacebar on my laptop to play the movie.

***

As the credits played at the movie's conclusion, Logan turned to me and said, "It was good."

"You really enjoyed the movie?" I asked, elevating my eyebrows.

"That hard to believe?"

"A lot of people might think postmodern cinema is pretentious."

He wiggled his eyebrows. "I'm not most people."

"I never said you were. I was just providing context."

"Understood."

I grabbed my Caramel Macchiato from the bed board and gulped the last drop. Yup. My taste buds were even more electrified than when I took my first sip. The caramel sticking to the bottom of the cup mixed that well with the remaining bit of espresso. Almost as if the beverage was heaven in a cup.

His eyes lit up. "Must be good if you're slurping the last drop."

Oops. I should have remembered my manners.

"Yeah." I tossed the Caramel Macchiato into the trash can next to my bed.

"Nice shot."

"Thanks. But I have never been one for sports."

"Neither have I," he said.

"What was your favorite part of the movie?"

Asking someone that question might have been typical when discussing a film or television show. But I couldn't helpful myself. I didn't need for my heart to beat any louder as a result of an awkward silence. I had no desire to win the record for most awkward silence of the year.

"I love the rewinding, because it's fascinating to see how one little detail can change an entire scenario," Logan said.

"Agreed. I'm just glad it had a happy ending."

"Me too."

"The movie also had a basic idea and wasn't as convoluted as some might think." I fanned myself with my T-shirt. Yeah. Summer wasn't dead even though there were only a few more days left in August.

His snickered. "Appearances aren't everything."

"It's like you took the words right out of my mouth."

"What do you want to do now?"

"We could go swimming. Or maybe you'd like to go grab a slice of pizza."

He looked me in the eye. "Yeah. Those are great options…"

"Something you wanna do?"

"I don't know. You tell me," Logan said.

Great. Logan had to use a double entendre just when I thought things were going well between us.

Sure. Making assumptions was dangerous. But people needed to trust their intuition, which meant there was a good reason why Logan hadn't taken his eyes off me. However, I shouldn't have criticized Logan for eye-fucking me. I hadn't averted my gaze either since my eyes were still on him.

Logan stared at me for another beat, but he didn't speak. Great. It was time to dial up the mystery by wondering what he currently thought.

He closed my laptop, making me almost scratch my chin.

I kind of knew there this situation with Logan was going, yet I wasn't psychic, and wondered if my hunch would come true.

Logan tucked a lock of my hair out of the way. His fingers then moved to my chin, and massaged my lower lip. Wow. I would have guessed he wanted to kiss me if I didn't know better.

He leaned in without any warning and pressed his lips

against mine. His hands were now wrapped around my cheeks. Although I wouldn't overthink this development. Nothing about Logan pricked my back hairs. There was also nothing wrong with Logan pursuing what he wanted. There was a difference between kissing someone and propositioning someone. Besides, I would never know what kissing Logan felt like unless I actually kissed him.

I closed my eyes after another beat. The kiss would be fleeting like everything else in life. And if I was gonna enjoy our current embrace, then I'd ignore the rest of the world. Logan and I didn't have forever, yet we had this moment. And said fact was amazing. It was something that the universe couldn't take from me.

CHAPTER 11

I was in the kitchen several mornings later, downing an entire glass of iced tea after going for a walk. Grandma would have even approved. She always started her day with a gigantic glass of iced tea and coffee despite Dad chastising about the habit encouraging her acid reflux.

Footsteps echoed, then someone entered the kitchen. I looked up. Sadie now stood in my kitchen and I wanted nothing more than to give her a hug. Even if doing so was rude given how sweat still clung to shirt and basketball shorts.

I clapped my hands together. "You're back!!!"

"Yup. And I want a hug regardless of whether you're sweaty."

"Sure." I gave her a quick hug, being careful to press too intensely against her.

Her face drooped. "Sorry about your grandmother."

"Thanks."

"I hope you know I would have flown back if I could…"

"Don't worry about it."

Having Sadie attend Grandma's funeral would have been nice, but she didn't need to prove herself. She made herself available to Facetime a couple of days after Grandma died, and that was good enough. Sadie could have blown me off because of being busy with her summer painting residency. Yet she extended herself by being a genuine friend.

Proving herself to me also would have also been a recipe for disaster. Grandma once told me about a college friendship ending because of being pretty certain the friend was flaky and the person getting tired of me being called out on the issue and always being "tested." Although at least the moment provided an extra chapter in Grandma's possible biography.

"How did you know to find me here?" I asked.

"I ran into your mom while she was gardening and she said you'd probably be in the kitchen hydrating."

"Tell me all about your painting."

"I'd rather talk about you," Sadie said.

"That's nice. However, the police still don't have any leads."

"I can't imagine how Theresa and Tony must feel since this isn't their first experience with death."

"Let's not even dwell on it."

"How's Tony?" She took out her hair tie, springing her wavy hair free. It extended a few inches past her shoulders. In fact, Sadie's hair had a certain elegance to it that someone should've taken a photo of it. Almost as if Sadie could've been a model. If that sort of thing interested her, that was.

Hold on. She just asked about Tony; not Theresa.

Her response meant digging. It wasn't like I wanted to be some nosy obnoxious person. Sadie mentioned Tony; not me. And I would have to find out what Sadie was getting at it. Because Grandma was the one who taught me the importance of finishing things.

"He gave me attitude at the funeral. But that's to be expected," I said.

She bit her nail. "I know why Tony is on edge."

"And why is that?"

"He told me he wanted to be more than friends before I left at the beginning of the summer."

I crossed my arms, giving Sadie a mock frown. "And you waited until now to tell me this? What were you thinking?"

Sadie giggled. "That's my point. I didn't know how to feel."

"Do you know what you're gonna say?"

Yup. I asked the tough questions. Doing so was part of being her best friend. It wasn't like I wanted to be a jerk and give her a hard time. I was just taking an interest in her life.

"No. But I've gotta figure it out ASAP," she said.

"We should have a party to welcome you home tonight," I said.

She shook her head. "We can't. My parents want to take me out to dinner. But maybe tomorrow night."

"Cool. Because I'm not passing up the chance to throw you a party."

"What about you? Meet any cute guys or girls?"

Damn. Sadie was smarter than she seemed because she made me the conversation's focal point.

So, I'd have to decide if I wanted to discuss Logan with Sadie. Two arguments could be made about whether I should mention Logan to anyone. On the one hand, I couldn't get too serious about Logan when we were still exploring our dynamic. Yet I needed someone to confide in, someone who I could reveal my insecurities too. Better I tell Sadie something bad than making a blunder with Logan.

Logan was also my first relationship, and needing guidance wasn't totally unrealistic or unreasonable. I would've done the same thing for Sadie if the situation was reversed.

"Well?" Sadie demanded.

"There's a new guy a couple of houses before you. He lives right across the street."

Her eyes beamed. "Tell me everything."

CHAPTER 12

I entered the kitchen the following morning, discovering Poppy and Uncle Brad standing by the stove. But I should have spent more time listening to what they were saying and less time pondering their physical placement. I never passed up the opportunity for escapism. Like when I was nine and eavesdropped on one of Grandma's phone calls with an author. The amusement was short-lived, though. Grandma discovered me and gave a stern lecture. Something about needing to mind my own business. Apparently, the telephone chat was sensitive since she informed an author that his book wasn't accepted by the acquisition's board.

Poppy hissed. "Everything will be fine."

"One of my guns is missing," Uncle Brad said.

"Don't look at me," she said.

"It could have been used to kill your grandma," he said.

I coughed, clearing the scratchiness from my throat. "Good morning."

Nothing wrong by interrupting their conversation, yet worrying must have been the only reason for the frown lines on Poppy's face. There was no way a twenty-something woman would want to start Botox so early in life. According to Grandma, that was. She used to bitch all the time about how Botox was expensive. Although I was supposed to keep that secret to myself. Something about Grandma not wanting to seem obsessed with plastic surgery.

Poppy tilted her head. "We didn't see you there, Casey."

I raised an eyebrow. "Everything okay?"

"One of my guns is missing from the safe," Uncle Brad said.

"I heard." I glanced towards the coffeepot. The "elixir" was still in the process of dripping down into coffeepot. In fact, the coffee was up to the halfway part in the coffee-pot. Although that was a minor detail compared to Poppy still having curled lips.

"You overheard our conversation?" Poppy asked.

I laughed. "We live in the same house."

"He's right, Poppy," he said.

Thank goodness for Uncle Brad. Arguing wouldn't help anyone. Not if we wanted to be united as a family during this difficult time.

Poppy sighed. "You're right. I shouldn't have gotten mad."

"No worries. It's a stressful time for all of us," I said.

"No shit," Uncle Brad said.

There was more to life than swearing. But something refreshing existed about Uncle Brad cursing. Sure. I loved Dad. But he couldn't have been more dissimilar to Brad if he tried. He almost never cursed in addition to how he always had a blazer, buttoned-down shirt, khaki pants, tie, black dress shoes, and combed back hair whereas Uncle Brad always dressed in a plaid or print patterned Polo shirt and shorts.

Poppy shifted her weight. "Don't fret too much, Brad. People lose things all the time. I'm pretty sure I'm missing an earring."

"That's terrible," I said.

She flipped her hair over her shoulders. "I'm sure it'll turn up."

"What if someone wants to frame me for the murder? Using my gun could go a long way to doing that," Uncle Brad said.

My eyes widened. "You don't think the killer broke into your safe and stole your gun, do you?"

"Yes," Uncle Brad stammered.

Poppy snorted. "Enough serious talk. We should be like Casey and enjoy life more."

"What are you talking about?" I asked.

"It's nothing to be ashamed of," she said.

I crossed my arms. "I'm not following?"

"I couldn't help overhearing your conversation with your dad about the new guy you're interested in," she said.

"Oh," I said.

"Don't get me wrong. I loved Grandma like everyone else. But we're going to be okay," Poppy said.

Criticizing Poppy would have been harsh. She hadn't destroyed Grandma's legacy. People just coped in different ways, and if she needed to be optimistic to survive, then I wouldn't begrudge her. I would have been furious if roles were reversed and someone told me I wasn't acting sad enough. Acting sad forever also would have dishonored Grandma's legacy. She was one of the most optimistic people I knew despite all of her quirks and trials and tribulations she endured.

The red light on the coffeepot disappeared after the dripping sound stopped echoing.

Fantastic. I could finally get my morning fix now.

I walked over the cabinet and grabbed a mug before pouring myself a more than generous cup. I then got a spoon and shuffled over to the fridge. Adding the half and half changed the coffee from black to a mocha color after I gave it a good stir. Yet I spit it out after tasting it.

Poppy glanced at me. "Something wrong?"

"Who made the coffee?" I asked.

Uncle Brad glanced at Poppy.

"I wanted to try a new brand," she said.

"No offense, but it's too bland," I said.

"Duly noted," Poppy said.

Uncle Brad pointed to his watch. "Time to get to the office, Poppy. Casey's father left half an hour ago."

Poppy groaned. "I'd rather spend the day at the beach."

He snickered. "That's what weekends are for."

Thank goodness I wasn't Poppy. She worked for Uncle Brad by helping with the accounting stuff for the publishing company, but that sounded just as dry as being a lawyer. No offense to them or anything. It wasn't like I shouted my opinion from a rooftop. I was just making a minor note to myself since there were more important things to worry about. Like getting a decent cup of coffee. Because gin was Grandma's oxygen, and coffee was mine.

CHAPTER 13

I exited the Starbucks in town on Main Street sometime later and bumped into someone. Wait. It was the disgruntled woman from Grandma's birthday party and funeral. I would have recognized her brown highlighted black hair anywhere as a result of admiring the contrast of both colors.

I bit my lip. "Sorry."

"It's not your fault. I wasn't paying attention to where I was going."

"We all have bad days." I continued staring at her.

She put her hands on her hips. "Can I help you with something?"

Yeah. Becoming a *New York Times* bestselling author and having a mansion in a tropical setting would have been fantastic. But she had no power to grant either wish since she wasn't a genie.

Although I should have been more concerned about the ring she dropped in church. Yup. It was time for another confession. I picked up the ring after she left and even tried tracking her down. Yet she disappeared like a magician demonstrating a magic trick in a matter of seconds. And it wasn't like I could put the ring in the lost and found box. The church didn't have one, and I was thus forced to hold onto the ring. Grandma would have encouraged me to sell the ring, though. She once found a fifty-dollar bill in a parking lot, and kept it. Dad even gave her a dirty look when Grandma told the story. Something about always wanting to be a boy scout and do the right thing.

"I don't know how to say this," I said.

She grinned. "I'm sure it can't be that bad?"

"You dropped your ring at my grandma's funeral, and I've been holding onto it."

She squealed. "I was wondering what I did with the ring."

"I can return it to you,"

"Sure. I'm staying at the Sandy Inn. Do you know where that is?"

I nodded. "Yes. It's a mile down the road from my family's mansion."

"Why don't you drop it by at two o'clock?" The lady opened her purse before taking out a pen and post-it. She then scribbled something down and handed it to me. "It's my cellphone number."

"Perfect," I said, taking the post-it from her.

***

The clunky sound of the engine halted the moment I took out the car key after pulling into my driveway.

I got out of my car before pressing a button on my car key. A beeping sound echoed, and the locks clinked shut. I wasn't being paranoid about locking my Mercedes. Sure. Spinderwood was one of those well-to-do suburban towns where people went to country club brunch on the weekend, teens agonized over getting an A instead of a A+, and overscheduled themselves, and residents took regular trips to Europe and other exotic locations. But one could never be too careful. According to Grandma, that was. She always mentioned how her parents were paranoid about security. Like with how they didn't just have the post office stop their mail when taking vacations. They also called their neighbors several times to make sure the house was still safe.

Logan waved at me from across the street, then I walked towards him.

I wouldn't even apologize for smiling. Getting to know Logan was something new and exciting to look forward to in my life after Grandma's death. And Grandma would have approved. Something about not waiting for life to happen, because she would have dwelled on the point. Being CEO of a publishing company meant understanding how passive characters wouldn't have people lining up at midnight when a book was released.

Logan waggled his eyebrows. "Another trip to Starbucks?"

"My cousin made bad coffee."

"The horror."

I remained silent.

He grinned. "The sunglasses are great on you."

Yup. He just flirted, because his eyes were still glued to me. I would have even said I would have melted if he continued staring at me. But I wouldn't complain. I—like everyone else—deserved an occasional win.

"Up to anything fun today?" I asked.

"Just thinking about our kiss."

Okay. Maybe I should have given myself more credit since Logan wasn't afraid of being flirtatious.

I blinked. "Really?"

"Is that a bad thing?"

"No. I was teasing."

"I hope I wasn't too forward."

Wow. There was a good chance that we were gonna

DTR. So, yeah. I had a legitimate reason for my heart almost leaping out of my chest. If I had my way, then nothing would ruin my potential relationship with Logan. Even if defining our relationship might be awkward.

I winked. "Don't worry about it."

"So…"

Logan was cuter than I realized. Apparently, he was comfortable enough with me that a gap in conversation didn't make his cheeks turn red. Even if I had better things to do than win an award for most awkward conversation.

"I'm having a welcome home party for a friend tonight. There will even be Margaritas. Unless you don't party, which is cool," I said.

Yeah. I backtracked. It wasn't that I wanted to be uncertain of myself. I just didn't want to seem conceded. I wasn't a mind reader, and didn't know how serious of a person Logan was. Especially with how we were getting closer and closer to the start of the school year. Like thing about SAT prep. Or how to maintain a 4.0

"What about your family?" Logan asked.

"They're going to a concert tonight," I said.

"Sure. Margaritas sound great. What time should I stop by?"

"It's TBD, but I'll text you."

"Cool." Logan gave me a quick kiss on the lips.

My skin once again burned at Logan's mere touch. I just didn't know how to describe the novelty even if the kiss only lasted a few seconds.

The short length was fine, though. Not everything had to be a nice romantic moment in the rain, because there'd be plenty of time for that later if I got my way.

***

"Thanks for returning my ring," said the lady a few hours later after I stepped into the inn's lobby.

"No problem."

The look of glee remained on her face. She then slid the ring onto her right index finger.

"It was a gift, and I don't know what I'd do if it was lost forever."

I snickered. Doing so had nothing to do with taking pleasure in someone else's misfortune. The universe just had a certain sense of humor. The woman wasn't the only one who lost something since Poppy might have misplaced her earring in addition to how Uncle Brad's gun was missing. Almost like losing stuff was contagious.

"You won't have to know now," I said.

"I'm Violet." She offered her hand.

"And I'm Casey."

She sucked in a breath. "I'm sorry for your loss."

"How did you know my grandma?"

"Through the publishing industry. She came close to accepting one of my manuscripts once and even let me resubmit it. But it still wasn't right for her. However, she gave me a referral to another publisher and we became friends anyway."

"Fantastic," I said.

My response was genuine. If Grandma helped Violet, that was a good thing. And Grandma of all people would have appreciated the beauty of strange or unexpected friendships by emphasizing how it made for an entertaining novel.

Violet wiped her right eye. "Do the police have any leads?"

"Not yet."

"I hope they find the killer."

"Do you mind if I ask a question?"

She shook her head. "Go ahead."

"You seemed upset the day of my grandma's birthday."

Yeah. The woman's emotional demeanor didn't escape me despite not being breaking news. Her anger was almost comparable to a sculptor chiseling away at a statue.

Except there was nothing left in Violet's case. Sure. She might not have had a breakdown. But the tightened muscles around her lips told me everything worth knowing about her that night.

"It was just a personal thing. Anyway, I'd love to chat, but I have things to do," she said.

"Have a good day." I was just about to leave the lobby when Violet sighed. Then, I whirled around.

"Maybe we could grab coffee at some point? Talking about your grandma might be helpful for both of us," she said.

I didn't hesitate. "Sure."

"Good. You have my number."

Making possible plans to hang out with a stranger was forward. Yet Violet couldn't have been some sort of closeted serial killer or deranged person. She would have made my skin crawl if she was terrible. Discussing Grandma with someone I never knew could also give me a new understanding about her, which might comfort me. Grandma would have even approved. And it wasn't because of getting to know someone who knew her. I was acting like an adult by expanding my social circle.

CHAPTER 14

"This was such a good idea," Sadie said after our "party" started.

Sadie, Tony, Theresa, Logan, and I were on my bedroom floor. We each had a red Solo cup in our hands, and there were two pitchers of Margaritas in front of us. There was a good chance that Dad would have disapproved if he were here. Something about how tequila was evil, which was bullshit. But Grandma wouldn't have given me shit about partying. Nope. She would have given me a standing ovation. Something about not being afraid to break rules. Because I was pretty sure the cops weren't about to walk through my bedroom door and bust us for underage drinking.

Tony grinned. "Agreed."

Theresa glanced at Sadie. "I'm glad you're back."

Sadie laughed. "You missed me that much?"

"Someone else can hang out with Casey besides me."

I frowned. "I'm sitting right here."

"You know what I meant," Theresa said.

Anyone else would have gotten one thousand lashes with a wet noodle. But Theresa was one of the few people who could tease me without offending me. She wasn't some malicious bully. Besides, Grandma would have appreciated my dynamic with Theresa. She said a small amount of teasing was healthy. Although I was pretty sure she preferred to do the teasing when it came to her friendships. Like that time when someone joked with Grandma slipping as her roots needed to bleached, and she didn't speak for the rest of evening. But she did run to the salon the next morning.

"I'm glad you guys included me," Logan said.

I glanced at Logan. "We'd be crazy not to."

Sadie guzzled the rest of her Margarita. "Looks like things are going well for you two."

"We practically just met," I said.

"No worries." Sadie squeezed Tony's hand.

I didn't miss one second of action, and would bring up Sadie's gesture. It was my turn to tease her now. Sure. I might have been guilty of being quirky with going off on tangents, but a fine line existed between being funny and being cruel.

"You two worked things out?" I asked.

"Yes," Tony replied before refilling his cup.

I took another swig of my drink. The mixture of the lime and tequila flavors jolted my mouth. Yeah. A Margarita was almost as good as a Caramel Macchiato. Maybe even better. But I would have denied my true opinion if someone asked me what I thought was better. Apparently, Starbucks was like the mafia. A person was in it for life. Because I didn't see myself breaking my coffee addiction at any point in the near future.

"I can't believe we got booze," Logan said.

"I have a fake ID," I blurted.

Sadie ran her fingers through her hair. "I wouldn't scream that from a rooftop."

"I have discretion," I said.

Tony turned to Logan. "What do you like to do?"

I gave Tony a dirty look. "Keep up! I already told you that he writes like me."

Tony might have been my cousin, but he deserved the award for most forgetful person of the year. Remembering Logan liked to write wasn't a complicated fact like dissecting the long-term foreign policy consequences of a treaty.

Sadie's jaw lowered. "I have a confession."

Theresa let out a loud laugh. "Did you kill someone?"

Sadie waved her hand through the air. "Don't be so dramatic. I was just talking about how I haven't even started preparing for the SAT's."

Theresa threw her hair over her shoulders with one flick of her head. "You have nothing to worry about. Artsy colleges are more flexible."

Sadie scratched her chin. "That's true."

"Does anyone know any good jokes?" I asked.

"You can't be serious," Sadie said.

"Fine. We don't have to tell jokes," I said.

"No shit." Sadie grabbed a handful of chips from the snack bowl next to the Margarita pitchers.

I drew in a breath. "But I do need to tell you guys one thing. Grandma was a teen mom because she gave a baby up for adoption when she was in high school."

Theresa clutched her necklace. "You're joking?"

"I wish," I said.

"You don't think the estranged child killed your grandma, do you?" Sadie asked.

I shrugged. "I don't know."

Tony gazed at his cup before chugging more of his drink. "The police can handle it."

"What Tony said," Sadie responded.

"Whatever," I said.

Moonlight continued trickling into my bedroom while the stars lit up the night sky. Wow. It was already getting late.

Whatever. No use in getting upset about something I had no control over. I was getting an ordinary teen moment, and I would enjoy every moment. I of all people appreciated how the universe was capable of surprising at any moment.

CHAPTER 15

Kicking and screaming was necessary a couple of mornings later. I so wanted summer vacation to end and endure nine agonizing months of school. It wasn't like I had anything better to do.

And no. Not wanting to go to school didn't make me a brat. I just had a bullshit meter. Sure. The general principle of school was commendable. But it was the place where creativity came to die for the most part. Yup. I stood by my statement. The school always pushed STEM and safe careers too much. No offense to the high school, but I had better things to do with my life. Not everyone could be good at math and science or have some boring safe career. Grandma would have even approved of my rationale. She always emphasized the importance of being consistent, which meant knowing I wanted to be a writer since I was five years old.

Life wasn't all misery, though. My opinion wasn't even because my high school humanized crocodiles as evidenced by the cartoon crocodile mascot I saw hanging on the school wall after I turned the corner in the hallway. I had reason to have a small spring in my step. Logan was only a few feet away from me at his locker.

"Hi," I said after walking up to him.

"Morning," Logan replied without turning around to face me.

"What's your first class?"

"Algebra 2."

"Me too. Who is your teacher?"

"Mr. Tripp." Logan glanced over his locker, which now had several notebooks resting on the top shelf. He closed the locker door before zipping up his backpack. The zipper squeaked as it made its way around the backpack perimeter.

"Me too. Maybe we could walk to class together."

"I actually have go straighten a few things out with my guidance counselor."

"No worries."

Logan walked away without another word or even asking what I was doing for lunch.

So, yeah. My heart might as well have been in my throat. Making a little bit of an effort before chatting with his guidance counselor wouldn't have killed Logan.

Hang on. There was no reason for me to assume Logan was mad at me. I wasn't the only thing going in his life as there must have been things going on before he met me. Yeah. That had to be it. Everything would be fine. I just knew it, and wouldn't worry until I had a reason to.

Theresa and Tony trekked down the hallway and walked up to me.

"Something wrong?" Theresa asked.

I grunted. "Logan did a whole 180."

"What did you do?" Theresa asked.

"Why do you assume I did something wrong?" I asked, stuttering.

Tony tugged at his backpack strap. "Have you met yourself?"

"Fair enough," I said.

She gave me a weak smile. "I'm sure it's nothing."

Good answer. I so needed to be told what I wanted to hear right now. Needing a little moral support was more than natural. It wasn't like I wanted Theresa to agree with everything I said or did. I just needed help dealing with whatever was going on with Logan.

I looked at Tony. "Where's Sadie?"

"She overslept," Tony said.

Wow. Perhaps Mercury was in retrograde. If I had been having a possible bad day, then that'd be one thing. But if Sadie was also dealing with a problem, then something was definitely wrong with the universe.

"I'm sure she'll be fine," Tony continued.

***

"I'm glad you accepted my offer," Violet said hours later after school.

We sat at a table outside in front of the Starbucks in town on Main Street since there were only a couple of clouds in the otherwise sunny sky. And I was gonna live despite how I usually didn't like to eat or drink outside. There were no flies or mosquitos buzzing around, so that was something to be thankful for.

I sipped my Caramel Macchiato. "I'm always happy to make new friends."

"There's one thing I have to tell you first."

Great. Talking to Violet couldn't be drama free.

"It's nothing bad," Violet said, biting her lip. "I just want to be honest."

"Tell me," I blurted.

"Your grandma had a baby when she was a teen."

"I know," I interrupted.

She pouted. "How do you know? Never mind. That doesn't matter."

Wait. Violet couldn't have been saying what I thought

68

she was going to say. There was just no way my hunch was correct.

"I'm that baby," she revealed. "Your grandma was my mother."

Okay. I needed to give myself more credit than I realized. My hunch was correct, and that meant I could have been psychic. So, maybe, just maybe, I would use my fake ID and buy a lottery ticket after finishing my conversation with Violet. If I was right about one thing—my hunch about Violet moments earlier—then I could have been right about something else.

I'd have to forget about possibly being blessed with a gifted intuition, though. For the moment, at least. I had a decision to make about what I'd do with the revelation about Violet being Grandma's daughter. And fast. Secrets had a way of being exposed whether a person wanted them to or not.

CHAPTER 16

I rang Logan's doorbell after coming home from coffee with Violet.

Talking to him wasn't about accusing him of anything. I wanted to know what the hell happened between us. I might not have dwelled on it, yet Logan hadn't just been icy with me when I approached his locker this morning. He hadn't said one word in Algebra 2 class in addition to other classes we had in common and during lunch. Besides, Grandma would have told me talking to Logan ensured I found find out what was bothering him. Something about how ambiguity was great for novels, but terrible for real life. Because I needed to know where things stood with Logan.

Damn. No answer.

So, I did the only thing I could do, and rang the doorbell again.

The door opened, revealing Logan.

He crossed his arms. "What do you want?"

"What gives with the icy treatment?"

Okay. Making a minor accusation was necessary. I couldn't dance around how our dynamic was awkward now. Although I hadn't accused him of being a terrible. I just wanted the truth. I refused to be one of those weak people I complained about when reading a book, or watching a show or movie.

His eyes bulged. "Excuse me?"

"You ignored me today at school."

Logan closed the door. "Keep your voice down."

"Don't tell me you wouldn't be angry if you were in my position?"

He pursed his lips. "No offense, but my whole world doesn't revolve around you."

I rolled my eyes. "I never said it did."

"Fine. You want to know the truth? My mom doesn't want me hanging out with you."

I almost snickered. But I didn't want to make this situation any worse regardless of the rage fuming through my body. Logan should have been his own person. Grandma would have even backed me up. Something about how being spineless wasn't an attractive quality.

"Why?" I spat.

A nearby squirrel grabbed an acorn before darting up a tree. Andi was almost envious of the squirrel. For a fleeting moment, that was.

Logan hesitated. "She thinks a relationship would invite too much drama."

Interesting. He used the word relationship. But the word wouldn't make me smile right now. Not when my dynamic with Logan seemed to be slipping away from me.

"Because?" I asked.

"Of your grandma's death," he mumbled.

Well, at least Logan hadn't mentioned dating me would've been too much because of how I was neurotic. I would've been even more pissed if he had.

I pouted. "That wasn't my fault."

"I know…"

I made a fist. Grandma's death was something I couldn't control.

"She also made me drop my internship," he said.

It was so great of Logan to share. He only confirmed what I thought. But it wasn't a nice thought. And that meant not dwelling on it no matter how tempting labeling him a coward was.

"Wouldn't you have had to drop it anyway because of school starting?"

He shook his head in a vigorous fashion. "Nope. They were going to let me work remotely."

"This situation sucks," I said.

Stating the obvious was the only thing worth doing. I just didn't know what to stay, because I couldn't ramble my way out of every situation.

He lowered his gaze. "You don't have to say that again."

The wind howled, pushing a mixture of red, orange, and yellow leaves into the distance. Wow. Another reminder of fall, which was another reminder of how Grandma's death would soon be fleeting like everything else in life. Whether I accepted the truth or not, life went on. And that meant it was only a matter of time before the rest of the world forgot about Grandma's death.

I sobbed. "There has to be something we can do."

"There isn't. My mother has always supported me, and I can't go against her."

I pointed my index finger at him. "I'm sorry, but you're a coward."

"Come again?"

"If it quacks like a duck and walks like a duck, it's a duck."

His nostrils flared. "You have no right to call me a coward."

"I just did." I walked away from Logan without another word. I said everything I could. Besides, talking in circles would only make my head throb. Logical fallacies didn't work well in real life, and only belonged in *Alice and Wonderland*.

***

"We need to talk," Mom said a few minutes later.

I just walked up to the house while Mom weeded her garden. Although she sported a tan hat, shirt, and shorts, which meant she should have gone on a hike. Telling Mom that she looked ready for a hike would have been mean, though, and I couldn't do that. I wasn't that cruel.

"What's up?" I asked.

"I found red cups in your room."

Shit. I should have remembered to clean up after my party.

I pressed my hands together. "I can explain."

"Don't bother." Mom yanked another weed with one swift motion.

"What do you mean?" I asked.

A fly buzzed near her face and she crushed it. "I'm not going to lecture you."

"You aren't?"

"Nope. I'm not happy you took advantage of how Poppy, your father, Uncle Brad, Aunt Rita and I all went to that concert. But I rather you drink at home if you want to drink."

Wow. I shouldn't have spent the previous minute cringing. Life always had a way of surprising me, and my current conversation with Mom was no exception.

Mom sighed. "Although I don't want you drinking on school nights."

I huffed out a sigh. "Fine."

"Anyway, enough serious talk. I noticed your scuffle across the street."

Interesting. Maybe Mom had more in common with Grandma than I realized. She was also capable of being dramatic.

"I wouldn't use that word," I said.

"Do you want to discuss it?"

I swallowed the lump in my throat. "Nope."

"You can if you want to. I won't judge."

Emphasizing not being judgmental might have happened a lot in life. But Mom's statement had a large degree of truth to it. Like that time when I was six and I got suspended from school for a day because I told off a teacher who was rude to me for no apparent reason. Because Mom hadn't even flinched when she picked me up in the principal's office.

"A relationship ended before it started," I said.

"Sorry, dear."

"It's whatever. You can't change anything."

My chest tightened while my next thought lingered in my mind. Venting to Mom might have been therapeutic. But mentioning my concern would make it real.

"What is it?" Mom asked.

"What if I can't fix things with Logan?"

"Then you allow yourself time to sulk before picking yourself up."

Her advice was simple, but seemed smart. Mom wasn't a bullshit artist because she hadn't told me everything would be okay. She gave me a minor dose of reality, which was necessary. False hope would have only made my body shudder because there was no sense in believing in something that couldn't be guaranteed. Grandma would have agreed with me. Emphasizing how one of the characters on *Pretty Little Liars* believed hope bred eternal misery was the only thing she liked about the show.

CHAPTER 17

I sat on a stool in the kitchen later in the evening after dinner, eating ice cream from the carton when footsteps scurried across the ground. And this evening was the one time I didn't care what Grandma would have thought of me. She would have lectured me about how using food as a coping mechanism was dangerous even though she would have reached for ice cream if roles were reversed. The footsteps soon grew louder and louder until my back hairs pricked up. Because I was the guy with goosebumps on my arms and back when someone spied on me.

I lifted my gaze. "What are you doing here?"

Logan exhaled a breath. "You have no right to call me a coward."

"You didn't answer my question."

"Tony let me in the house, but that's not the issue."

I dug into the ice cream with my spoon. Yet the vanilla ice cream wasn't as creamy and sweet like did in the past. Figures. There was nothing like a disastrous love life to ruin a mood since I put too much stock into our interactions. I was only a teenager, and should have waited a few years before worrying about finding the love of my life.

I glared at him. "Arguing isn't going to accomplish anything."

"I don't care."

"I'm not gonna apologize for calling you a coward."

He crossed his arms. "I don't know what you want me to do."

"You know what I want you to do. You just won't do it."

"We had this discussion already," Logan said.

I snorted. "You're the one who came to my house uninvited."

I just had to be blunt. I refused to be a pushover since I deserved better than what Logan had given me.

"You don't understand how difficult this is," Logan added.

I stood. "If you came here for sympathy, you'll be disappointed. It's not my job to prop you up."

"Fuck it." Logan pulled me closer before I blinked.

His lips approached mine before lingering for a beat. Great. There was a good chance that I would die from anticipation.

He looked me in the eye, making me wonder if he noticed my defeated look I had ever since Grandma's death. His lips soon pressed mine, and he placed a hand on each of my cheeks.

Closing my eyes wasn't odd to me even if that might have been some people's go to move in a crisis. Savoring every second of the kiss was my only option. Because there was no telling when the next bad thing would happen.

"You can't send mixed messages," I said after pulling back.

Sure. I wouldn't lie. I enjoyed the kiss and hoped to do more than kissing. But I couldn't do ambiguous situations. I deserved someone who was comfortable with me.

Logan also should have known better than to waste both of our time.

"I know," Logan said.

"Where does this leave us?" I asked.

"I like you as more than a friend regardless of my mom's feelings."

"Same. And I didn't mean to hurt your feeling by calling you a coward."

His Adam's apple throbbed. "I understand."

My iPhone beeped, and I pulled it out of my pocket.

I challenged anyone not to have a lowered jaw after looking at the breaking news alert I just read. The police arrested Violet for murdering Grandma after an anonymous tip led them to discovering the gun in her room at the Sandy Inn. The bullet was a match for the ones in the gun that killed Grandma.

Advanced notice before finding out on the news would have been nice, though. Even if letting my family have prior notice would have been too easy. Life just always had to be complicated. Although Grandma would have lectured me about criticizing drama since she believed all novels without conflict were terrible.

Logan squeezed my shoulder. "What's wrong?"

"There's been a break in my grandma's murder."

CHAPTER 18

I approached my locker the following morning at school while numerous thoughts about Violet swirled in my mind. I just didn't understand how she could be responsible for Grandma's murder.

Sure. I had no problem conceding how I knew nothing about her apart from my brief interactions with her. But being a writer meant observing people. It wasn't like Violet raised any immediate red flags. Yet the police had found the murder weapon in her room at the inn.

I did my locker combination and my locker clinked open after another beat. Although my mind continued dwelling on Violet. I just didn't want to believe she was responsible for killing Grandma. Being related to Grandma meant believing denial was always preferable than dealing with truth when it came to the truth.

Someone's hands covered my eyes.

"Surprise!" yelled someone.

Hmmm. A mixture of a sweet and earthly scented deodorant wafted through the air. And that only meant one person. Logan now stood behind me, which was great. Because anyone else putting their hands over my eyes would have just seemed sketchy.

I smiled. "Someone is feeling frisky."

"Get your mind out of the gutter."

"I was kidding."

"I know. Anyway, there's something I wanted to ask you."

I put the last textbook into my locker before closing it and zipping up my backpack. "I hope it isn't bad."

"Nope. I was just wondering if you wanted to go out on a date tomorrow night?"

I had to have been having a fever dream. Logan couldn't have just asked me if I wanted to go out on a date. Not because I didn't deserve to be happy. But because I always glanced over my shoulder, wondering when the next bad thing would happen. It wasn't my fault how the universe loved making me it's victim.

My grin widened. "That'd be great."

***

Saying I visited the Spinderwood County Jail wouldn't enhance my biography someday. But I had to suck up my pride and visit the jail after school if I wanted answers from Violet.

"I was wondering if you'd visit me," Violet said while shackles covered her wrists and ankles in addition to how she sported an orange jumpsuit.

We were seated at one of the tables in the visitor's room.

I furrowed my eyebrows. "Really?"

"Yeah. You seem nice."

"Did you do it?" I whispered, almost being unable to speak. There was just something damning about asking such a direct question.

She giggled. "You don't waste time."

"Do you wanna know what I think?"

She nodded.

Good. I didn't have time to argue with her, and she would hear what I had to say whether she wanted to or not.

"I don't think you did it," I blurted. "I bumped into you before going into the house. That would have meant you went around back and snuck into the house and shot her. Then, you would've had to somehow escape before I discovered the body."

"You're clever."

"I don't want a compliment. I just want the truth."

Violet grunted. "You're right; I didn't do it. But I'm not Mrs. Perfect."

"I know about your letter."

"Yup. She eventually reached out to me and we even became friends. But I needed money to pay some credit card debts. Yet she wasn't liquid. That wasn't my biggest gripe, though."

"What do you mean?"

She started crying. "I went into the mansion before bumping into you. We got into an argument because she changed her mind about introducing me to the family."

My jaw lowered. "She wanted to introduce you to the family?"

"That's what I said."

"Forgive me. I don't mean to sound stupid, it was just shocking."

"Did you know you were a suspect when we had coffee?" I asked.

She whipped her head back and forth. "No. I was running an errand when they searched my room at the inn. They had a warrant."

"Do you have an alibi?"

"Yes. I met up with my ex-husband because he agreed to give me a loan," she revealed. "It was literally within less than five minutes of chatting with your grandmother. My ex-husband met me in my car, which was parked near your house."

Interesting. The woman wasn't afraid to go to her ex for a loan. But I couldn't judge her. I had no idea what it was like to be in her position.

"Why don't you tell the police?" I asked.

Her eyes shifted to the table's wooden surface. "You don't know how embarrassing it is that my books haven't been selling as well as I thought they would. Besides, my ex-husband cheated on me, and you don't know how humiliating asking for his help is."

My lips quivered. "That type of thing takes time. Anyway, you can't seriously wanna go to jail because of your pride?"

"It's my life. Promise you won't tell anyone."

"Why be honest with me? You don't even know me."

"I have nothing left to lose because I'll probably go to jail for a long time thanks to my shitty public defender," Violet said.

"How did you not know the gun was in your inn room?"

"It was found under my bed. I mean, I don't know about you, but how often do you see look at the carpeting under your bed?"

I pouted. "I could get you a lawyer."

"That's okay. But thanks for listening. It's more than most people are willing to do."

Her words lingered in my mind despite how obvious they were. My body then shuddered. Something cruel existed even though her idea was basic. Perhaps it was the writer in me that appreciated the sadness of Violet having nothing.

CHAPTER 19

"How are you doing, honey?" Mom asked several hours later.

We stood in the kitchen, waiting for her Apple Pie to be ready. Because that was the one good thing about fall approaching. There was nothing like the scent of cinnamon, baking apples, and sugar wafting through the kitchen. Even if Grandma would have lectured me about how consuming too many calories was dangerous.

"Fine," I said.

"You don't have to put up a front with me. You must have feelings about Grandma's killer being arrested."

Mom meant well. But I was seventeen—not a little kid. I didn't need someone to manage my feelings. I would have reached out for support if my feelings got too difficult to manage. I wasn't an idiot and understood the importance of not bottling up emotions.

"I would rather not rush to judgment," I said.

She tucked a lock of hair behind her ear. "That's big of you."

"It's the truth. We don't know anything about the women."

Her gaze narrowed. "Why would you say that?"

"I want to spend less time focused worrying about others and more time on myself."

"I can't say your father feels the same way. He's focusing on how the police should have kept us more involved. He's even talking about suing…"

Mom pursed her lips. "I'm just glad the police think the woman stole Uncle Brad's gun and aren't trying to implicate him in this."

"That's a fair point."

The oven chimed.

Mom's eyes lit up. "Wonderful! The pie is ready."

Minor happiness filled my body. For a moment, that was. There was some innate comfort about food. Like a snack or meal was something to look forward to no matter how shitty life. So, maybe, just maybe, the Apple Pie was exactly what I needed for distracting myself about Violet currently being in jail.

***

"Thanks for helping me pick an outfit for the picnic," I said the following afternoon while standing in my bedroom.

Theresa giggled. "No need to thank me. I live and breathe fashion."

Yeah. I had to write down Theresa's comment. It would make for a nice sassy line in my writing someday.

"Old habits," I said.

Theresa snapped her fingers. "Eureka!"

"What is it?"

"I know what you should wear." Theresa handed me a matching salmon colored Polo shirt and pair of shorts.

I raised my eyebrows. "You don't think it's too much?"

"Don't be ridiculous. It's genius."

"Yeah. Okay."

She put her hands on her hips. "Why? Would you rather wear something else?"

"Don't put words in my mouth."

She cracked her knuckles. "I'm glad you trusted me to pick at out an outfit."

"Why wouldn't I?"

"Sadie is back."

I snickered. "We can still be friends. Besides, you really stepped up for me this summer."

"My pleasure."

Wanting to be friends with Theresa wasn't about being polite. I had no reason to "dump" her. She was a nice enough person. Her interest in fashion also meant she was creative like me. Besides, I had nothing to gain by shutting her out. Life wasn't a series of absolute events. I had plenty of time to be friends with both Theresa and Sadie. It wasn't like someone would put a gun to my head and make me choose which one I wanted to be friends with.

***

"Is something wrong with your sandwich?" Logan asked sometime later.

A blanket covered the grass where we sat in the park. The park was almost empty, and the wind wasn't making the trees bob about too much. That made me almost thank the universe for one fleeting second. I deserved to have something go right in light of everything I had been through lately.

"No. It's good," I said.

Logan lifted the picnic basket's top and pulled something out. "I even got Tiramisu for dessert."

How sweet of him. He remembered how I told him Tiramisu was my favorite dessert. Grandma often preached to me about the importance of remembering little details. She once told me about how one of her past boyfriends didn't know what her favorite type of pasta was.

I grinned. Maybe, just maybe, making Logan believe I was happy would make me happy. It wasn't like I wanted the date to bomb. I just couldn't help having a lot on my mind as a result of Violet's arrest. Lying would have entailed not mentioning my stomach twisting in ten different directions, and I couldn't do that. Violet being locked up seemed unfair. And it wasn't like she could have a bail hearing because of the local court being backed up.

His eyebrows inched up. "I'm really trying."

"I didn't say anything."

"Is your uneasiness about your grandmother?" Logan asked.

"Yes," I whimpered.

He patted my shoulder. "You can discuss the case if it'll make you feel better."

Interesting. Perhaps I was too quick in judging my date with Logan. It wasn't like I would always talk about myself.

"I would rather talk about you," I said.

"That's kind of you."

"Writing anything new?"

Yeah. I put Logan ahead of myself by taking an interest in his life. It was what Grandma would have wanted. Because if she could visit me as a ghost she would have made some dramatic comment about being disappointed in me for being too afraid to live my life.

CHAPTER 20

"You'd be proud of me," I said the next morning after turning the corner in the school hallway. Sadie glanced at me. "Why is that?"

"I put Logan above me."

"How so?"

"I took in interest in him as opposed to ranting about my concerns about Grandma's murder."

She pulled her backpack strap tighter, as if she needed a distraction. "Everything okay?"

"I don't wanna discuss it."

She bit her lip. "Fair enough."

"How are you liking the new school year?"

"I dropped Physics and swapped it with an art class," Sadie said.

I chuckled. "Your guidance counselor let you do that?"

"Why? Is that so hard to believe?"

"You need three years of science to graduate."

She giggled. "I'm gonna take AP Environmental Science next fall."

"Smart. I might take that class too."

"Desperate to avoid Physics?"

I rolled my eyes. "You should know better than to ask that question."

She flipped her hair over her shoulders. "Tony and I have been texting a lot."

"Please don't make my ears bleed."

Her jaw trembled. "I need you to be honest about something."

"I'll try."

Sadie gave me a dirty look. "I'm serious, Casey."

Being my best friend meant I should have been honest with her. But I couldn't help my pulse ringing in my ears. Worrying was natural in light of everything that happened in life over the last few weeks. Like with Grandma dying, my drama with Logan, and worrying if the police arrested an innocent person.

Yes. I went there. Being respectful of the police wasn't mutually exclusive with blind loyalty. At least according to Grandma. She was the expert Democrat of the family. She used to take her politics seriously since she always had MSNBC on in her office at work. Uncle Brad even tried to start an argument with her one time by switching to FOX. But Grandma pretended she hadn't heard him and continued smiling and drinking her Gin and Tonic.

"What are you getting at?" I asked.

"Are you sure you're doing okay in light of your grandmother's death?"

I didn't know whether to laugh or scream. Having a considerate best friend was something to be thankful for. But I wasn't the emotional equivalent of glass. Grandma's death was terrible, and I thought about her every single day. However, I had a support system. And that was enough. I would mention Grandma's death if I wanted to discuss it more.

I nodded. "Yes, I'm fine."

The bell rang.

Great. Another day. Another Algebra 2 class. Because I so wanted to spend the rest of my life thinking about math.

***

I did something gutsy after school and drove to the Spinderwood police station. Doing so wasn't about being arrogant. I just had to speak to one of the detectives on Grandma's murder case.

Butting into Violet's case made me nosy, but I couldn't help myself. She didn't have it in her to kill Grandma, and I would have bet my life on it.

I pulled the key out the ignition before getting out of my Mercedes. I did the same thing I always did, and locked my car before shuffling towards the police station's entrance.

I pushed the door open and trekked into the lobby. A man with short curly hair sat at the reception desk. He was also rather plump because it seemed like he he shirt and pants would rip if he sneezed. I had enough restraint to keep any comment to myself. Unlike Grandma. There was no reason to be cruel by bringing up someone's weight.

He lifted his gaze off his computer. "Can I help you with something?"

"I would like to speak to Detective Johnson. It's about Rose's murder," I said.

The man rubbed his mustache. "Absolutely."

The elevator hummed a few minutes later. The doors opened, revealing Detective Johnson—the detective that interviewed me the night Grandma died. She then walked over to me. Yet she didn't even bother smiling. And I was pretty sure Grandma would have mentioned having an uptight look meant she needed to get laid. That was one of her favorite comments to make.

She beamed her eyes. "What can I do for you?"

"I don't mean any disrespect, but I think you arrested the wrong person. You don't have to take my word for it. Ask Violet's ex-husband. She's too ashamed to admit the truth, but she had an alibi for the night my grandma died."

CHAPTER 21

A couple of mornings later, I exited my Mercedes in the school parking lot.

Streams of sunlight radiated from the otherwise almost cloudy sky while wind roared, pushing an empty soda can down the parking lot. And I would have some comment about how today would be a great if I were an optimist. But even I wasn't foolish enough to waste my time. I would just hope today was a draw. Nothing good. Nothing bad. Because I could live with that.

Something buzzed.

Judging from the vibrations, it was my iPhone.

"Hello?" I asked after taking a quick glance at the caller ID before accepting the call. Wait. It was Violet's number.

"It's me."

"I know."

"What do you want? I have first period in 15 minutes," I said, raising my voice.

Fuck. I shouldn't have been so harsh. I defended Violet and had no reason to get mad at her. Grandma would have been a little intense, though. Something about the importance of having good timing.

"The police released me," Violet said.

I laughed, causing brief static. "I figured that out for myself."

"Thanks for going to the police."

"You aren't mad at me?" I asked.

She sighed. "Nope. You helped me when I couldn't help myself."

"I didn't mean to overstep."

"Forget about it," she said.

"Did you just call to thank me?"

"Sorry. I was wondering if you would want to stop by for a celebratory drink after school? We need to talk about something."

I snorted. "You know I'm not 21, right?"

"No need to discuss semantics. A smart guy like must have a fake ID. Although I'm serious. I have my suspicions about who killed your grandmother. I don't want to become a target, but you deserve to know the truth. Someone walked into her bedroom after I left."

Sweat clung to my forehead. There was no way Violet said what she had. She had to be mistaken. She couldn't know who killed Grandma because I wasn't prepared to deal with the truth. Besides, the universe wasn't so giving. And that meant Grandma's killer wouldn't have been handed to me on a silver platter.

"Can't you tell me over the phone?" I asked.

"That wouldn't be smart."

"Fine."

"I'm leaving town tomorrow, but you deserve to know the truth," she said.

I wiped the sweat from my forehead with my free hand. "Are you saying the person who killed Grandma framed you by putting the gun in your room at the inn?"

She remained silent for the longest time. "Probably."

"4:30 P.M. work for you?" I asked.

"Perfect. You can meet me outside my inn room. It's room 313, and I'll tell the receptionist I'm expecting company."

Fuck it. There was still one question I had to ask no matter how difficult it was.

"Do I know the possible killer?" I asked.

She didn't speak. Not after first. Her breathing just increased, causing additional static on her end of the line.

"Yes," she said.

A knocking sound echoed. But it wasn't from my end.

Violet hissed. "Someone is at the door, but I look forward to seeing you later."

"Sounds good."

"Okay. Bye."

***

I returned home from school later in the day and decided to go into the kitchen to have some iced tea. Doing so was the mistake of the century, though. And no. My comment wasn't an attempt to make light of serious situation. Aunt Rita, Uncle Brad, Poppy, Mom, and Dad were already in the kitchen. But it wasn't their presence that made my stomach tighter than my brain trying to solve a difficult math equation. Nope. Their stern expressions were the real reason for my increased pulse. Being related to Grandma meant at least bringing up the possibility of facing an inquisition.

"Did someone die?" I asked.

Shit. I should have known better than to make that remark in light of Grandma's death. but I couldn't help myself. A wake might as well have been going on in my kitchen. And it wasn't even because of their grim facial expressions. They all sported at least one item of black clothing.

"How can you say that?" Dad asked.

Poppy glared at Dad. "Don't be harsh. He's a teen and must be under a lot of pressure."

"Don't make excuses for him," Mom snapped.

"It's just so awful," Aunt Rita said.

I folded my arms. "What the fuck is going on?"

Mom's eyes widened. "Watch your language."

"That's the least of our problems," Poppy said.

Thank goodness for Poppy. I just didn't understand the contempt radiating from their eyes since I didn't do anything that would have offended anyone.

"There was a leak to the press." Uncle Brad took his glasses off. He ran the cold water and put his glasses under the oozing stream before turning the faucet off. Uncle Brad then grabbed a cloth from his pocket and wiped his glasses.

"What kind of leak?" I asked.

Dad grimaced. "Someone told the press about the child your grandmother gave up for an adoption was a teen. It's all over the local news, and they made the connection that the woman was Violet."

My lips curled. "Don't look at me."

"We know you visited Violet in county jail," Mom said, frowning.

"What proof do you have?" I asked.

"They called home," Dad revealed. "I'm mean, don't you realize we've had enough trouble with the police asking Brad about how his gun ended up being the murder weapon? We can't skate by on luck forever."

I gave them a dirty look. "I didn't leak anything to the press."

Mom sighed. "We didn't say you did."

Figures. Mom had to backslide. Typical nice behavior. One minute she was furious, and the next she calmed down.

"We're just concerned about you visiting a criminal," Mom continued.

"An alleged criminal," Poppy interrupted.

I screamed. "I don't have to stand here and listen to this. I did nothing wrong, and don't need to defend myself."

Storming out of the kitchen wouldn't have won me any awards for gentleman of the year. But it was the only move I had. The worrier in me meant not being late to my afternoon meeting with Violet. Our impending chat was the most important thing I could do. Discovering the truth might help me win the approval of my family again. Doing so was worth a try, at least. It wasn't like my life could get worse.

CHAPTER 22

I took the stairs after arriving at the inn because taking the elevator was about as appealing as being surrounded by thousands of spiders. Sure. There was a good chance everything would be fine. But I couldn't risk that one to five percent chance of something going wrong. I so needed the elevator to come to a halt while sweat dripped down my face and my heart thumped faster inside my chest. No thanks. My pulse rang in my ears loud enough with worrying about who killed Grandma in addition to wondering if my relationship with Logan would remain perfect.

I would've knocked on Violet's door was pointless, yet it was unlocked.

Yeah. A lump lingered in my throat because Violet's unlocked room didn't make any sense. And Grandma would have made some comment about something maybe going horribly wrong if she were here. But I would wait to reserve judgement until getting concrete proof that something was wrong.

Going inside the room wasn't the smartest thing because I didn't know what I would discover. But it was the only option I had.

"Fuck." I clapped my hand over my mouth. Violet's body was hanging from the ceiling fan—which was near the bed on the right side of the room with a rope around her neck—and attached to the center of the fan. I wouldn't even question how a ceiling fan could support a human. Violet couldn't have weighed more than one hundred pounds and been taller than five-three. So, Violet using a gigantic ceiling fan to attempt suicide wasn't completely illogical. My gaze shifted. A folded piece of paper was on the table between the two beds.

No. No. No. Violet couldn't have been dead. Real life wasn't supposed to be dramatic like pop culture.

I scurried over to the table. Violet was probably dead, and I had to read what the note said. Doing so was the fastest way for ensuring answers.

I unfolded the piece of paper, then read the note:

I just had to kill myself. I lied and manipulated Casey in addition to getting my ex-husband to agree to lie for my alibi. I really killed my mother because I was pissed she didn't introduce me to her family. It also didn't help that she wasn't liquid and couldn't help me out in my financial pinch.

I'm so sorry,

Violet

Violet couldn't have committed suicide. I believed her when she told me she didn't kill Grandma. She also didn't seem to have it in her to kill someone. This situation was one of the times I would have to play devil's advocate, though. I didn't really know her and couldn't be sure what thoughts were going through her.

My chest expanded and contracted while my breathing increased. The room also might as well have been spinning like when I discovered Grandma's corpse the night of her birthday party. I had to act fast because I couldn't implicate my family in another scandal. I suffered enough from the intense looks on everyone's faces when I was in the kitchen earlier today. But I wasn't a coward. There was nothing I could do to save Violet.

I exhaled one more deep breath before leaving the room.

My mind soon drifted. The killer could have been the person knocking on the door during my earlier phone conversation with her. Although Violet's words were important regardless of her dying. She mentioned I might have known the killer, which was enough to give me goosebumps. Because another one of Grandma's opinions was true. The universe didn't only fuck with people. It also had a sick sense of humor. And that meant I could have known the killer without actually knowing I knew the killer.

CHAPTER 23

Someone tapped my back several days later after I finished stuffing my backpack with what I needed for my morning classes.

I closed my locker door before turning around.

Great. Logan stood in front of me.

He smirked. "Hi, sexy."

As if I needed another reason to drool over my hot boyfriend. Because I so wanted to resemble a love-sick fool. Yet I couldn't help being intoxicated by Logan. He was the first person I ever dated. So, I'd naturally get carried away in the intensity of the romance.

"I thought we should talk," Logan continued.

I frowned. "Did I do something wrong?"

"No. I just heard about Violet getting out and then killing herself."

"I can't talk about it." I bit my lip. A metallic sensation filled my mouth. My pulse soon vibrated in my ears loud enough that I just had to bite my lip.

His face drooped. "Please don't shut me out, Casey. I

thought we were in a good place."

Damn. He had to give me the benefit of the doubt. It wasn't like I could tell him how I discovered Violet's corpse. I just couldn't implicate Logan in the situation. The false sense of trouble when the police called home again to keep my family updated after one of the inn maids discovered Violet's dead body the following morning after I came across it was bad enough.

Logan huffed. "There's something you aren't telling me."

I exhaled a breath. "I can't discuss it."

He squeezed my hand. "There's nothing you can't tell me."

"It'd unravel too much."

"You're scaring me."

I sobbed. "I'm sorry. I can't do this."

"I'm not gonna judge you. I just want you to be honest with me."

I made a fist. For once, I agreed with the expression, "I don't know." The saying—which Grandma used a lot when she was alive—seemed fitting. Violet was free one minute and dead the next.

He parted a lock of my hair to the side. "Something is bothering you."

I cried even louder. "You just don't understand. It's too complicated."

"Casey, please!"

"I'm sorry, but I just can't do this."

He pursed his lips. "Fine. But don't say I didn't try."

CHAPTER 24

Rain splattered onto the ground hours later at lunch while I sat at one of the tables near the high school's main entrance. But I wasn't a masochist. There wasn't a chill in the air—it was humid. The rain also wasn't pounding the ground. It was only drizzling, and wouldn't kill me. I also smiled because of one of Grandma's strange philosophies. She would have commented about rain being romantic or preferable to sunny weather. Like that time when she was nervous giving a speech at an outdoor writer's conference and threw a party when it was canceled due to heavy rain.

"What are you doing in the rain?" called out a voice.

I cocked my head. Sadie stood next to me. Great. As if I didn't feel awkward enough. Nope. My best friend had to be here.

She sat next to me. "Tell me everything."

I hung my head lower. "You don't wanna know."

"You can tell me anything."

I pouted. Yup. I was the guy who had to be emotional, and I wouldn't apologize. Dealing with Grandma's death, Violet's death, and my relationship with Logan was too much. I was only seventeen, and deserved some fun.

"I fucked things up with Logan," I said.

She furrowed an eyebrow. "What are you talking about?"

I gasped. "There's a lot you don't know about my grandmother's murder."

She grabbed my hand. "Just tell me. I won't judge."

Sadie just had to say that. And I wasn't being harsh. People always pretended to be more open-minded than they were. It was a fact. Like with how Grandma once pretended to be okay with dating a Republican several years ago even though she wasn't. Something about how the man was hot and she could pretend to overlook his obvious flaw if meant having a more exciting love life.

"I can't tell you anything, but I want to tell Logan the truth," I said.

She sucked in a breath. "What can I do for you?"

Being honest with Logan would be worse than solving a complex equation in Algebra 2 class. But it had to be done. Nothing could jeopardize our relationship, and I had to swallow my pride. Doing so was the only option to save my relationship with Logan. Grandma was also the one who once mentioned most relationships were defined by at least one larger than life moment. Like what broke up her relationship with the previously mentioned Republican man who she dated. He made some comment about gin tasting like gasoline, and that was more than enough to make Grandma show him the exit.

***

I sat at a booth at the Spinderwood Diner hours later with a slice of Apple Pie and a cup of coffee in front of me.

The placard on the door chimed, and footsteps squeaked against the floor.

Logan froze after arriving at my booth. Great. I wanted nothing more than to be kept in suspense. It wasn't like I had enough problems. He then continued staring at me for a beat before I gesticulated for him to sit down. Because I could only take so much hovering.

I grinned. "Thanks for coming."

"No problem." He removed his leather jacket, and put it down next to him.

Logan rested his free hand under his chin. "I'll make this easy for you."

"What are you talking about?"

"I know you're keeping something from me."

I scowled. "What makes you say that?"

"You're an open book."

"If you say so."

His eyebrows swung up. "Tell me what's on your mind."

I shook my head, sobbing. "Telling you will change everything."

He grabbed my hand. "Doesn't matter. Nothing will jeopardize our relationship.

I grabbed my fork, and broke off a bit of Apple Pie. The mixture of the sweet and tart flavors jolted my taste buds while the revelation hit me. Fall was practically here. Although fall or winter still couldn't arrive. The weather had to be warm as long as possible. I needed to buy new clothes for winter, and I refused to have the weather be ahead of my schedule.

More tears fell down my face. "I'm gonna sound crazy."

"I don't think you're crazy." He held my hand tighter.

The waitress shuffled over to us.

"Can I get you anything?" she asked.

Logan grinned. "I'll have a slice of Apple Pie and a cup of coffee."

She scribbled down the order in her notepad. "Sure

thing."

"Thanks," he said.

The waitress left, as fast as she first appeared. And it was now just Logan and I.

"I don't think Violet killed my grandma regardless of what the suicide note said."

"You don't?" he asked.

"Nope." I sipped my coffee. Thank goodness it was no longer scolding hot. Coffee was meant to be enjoyed, not something to wait an eternity to cool off.

He nodded. "I'm listening."

I coughed, clearing the scratchiness from my throat. "I think someone killed Violet and made it look like a suicide. She had no reason to kill herself. She wanted to leave town after talking to me. Because she says another person met with Grandma after she did"

"I see."

I had another bite of Apple Pie before responding. "I spoke to her before she died. Someone knocked on her inn room door, and I think that person killed her. It makes sense. I discovered her dead several hours later. But I couldn't say anything without implicating myself."

He grabbed my hand, electrifying every cell in my body. Yup. I squealed over having another guy rub his hand against mine. This evening might not have been one of those larger than life moments Grandma mentioned. But I wasn't a prude, and appreciated affection —whether it was big or small.

Logan gazed into my eyes. "I believe you."

"You do?"

"Yup. And that's why I'm gonna help you solve your grandma's murder. She was my friend. Besides, we deserve closure."

Perfect. Things were better than ever with Logan since we were gonna play detectives. And I wasn't exaggerating because I wasn't oblivious to the perks of having a partner in crime. I was able to be honest with someone, and that was good. I didn't deserve to be alone because life was too short. Besides, I couldn't solve Grandma's murder by myself. I wasn't a jack of all trades like Grandma. And in my case, that meant having no idea where to start the investigation now that Violet was dead.

CHAPTER 25

I was in the middle of finishing Algebra 2 homework a couple of days later at one of the tables in front of the high school when Logan approached. I could have accused him of having a strut in his step if I wanted to get technical. But it wasn't like Logan always drank the Kool-Aid by believing in sunshine and rainbows 24/7. Nope. Logan wasn't one of those people who lived in a bubble, and believed life existed in a vacuum. And said fact was a good thing. I didn't know what I would've done if Logan wasn't capable of having at least one negative thought.

"Hi, babe," Logan said before giving me a quick kiss, and sitting next to me.

Babe.

The word had a nice ring to it. Because I had now gotten the swoon worthy relationship I always wanted. Even if analyzing every little detail made me obsessive. Personality traits were like bad style choices, though. Owning them was the only way to make them work. And I had Grandma to thank for the insight. Grandma's stylist once dyed her hair so dark that it almost looked brown a couple of years ago, yet she hadn't flinched when telling the story. Almost as if the issue resembled a squashed mosquito.

"You seem extra happy today." I scribbled one more thing down in my notebook before closing both it and my textbook.

He frowned. "That a bad thing?"

I chuckled. "Just making an observation."

"You aren't wrong."

"Excuse me?"

"I thought a lot about your grandma."

I raised an eyebrow. "You have?"

"I think we should search her bedroom again."

"And why is that?" I asked.

Nope. I wasn't giving Logan a hard time. Knowing what made him think about searching Grandma's bedroom would have been helpful. I had been scratching my chin for endless hours over the last couple of days ever since Logan agreed to join me and play detective. But I came up with nothing.

"The police might have missed something," Logan said.

His reasoning seemed logical. Going through Grandma's bedroom seemed to be the easiest thing to do in light of being uncertain about what happened to her. And I would have taken a second to give myself grief if I had a moment to spare. But I didn't, and just had to be glad Logan could be clever for both of us.

I winked. "Maybe you should be a cop."

Yup. Logan wasn't the only one who flirted well. I dialed up the charm too. It wasn't like I wanted to sleep with Logan right here in front of the high school. I just wanted to add an age appropriate amount of spice and mystery to our relationship. Even Grandma would have approved. She was never afraid to be saucy. Like that time a year and a half ago when she was convinced the waiter was flirting with me. She begged me to test the theory, but I pleaded with her to let it go.

"That's okay. I already know I want to be a young adult writer," Logan said.

"It was a joke."

Logan wiggled his eyebrows. "I know."

"It still bugs me how the police aren't even questioning the suicide note or logistics of Violet killing herself."

He squeezed my hand. "Relax. I believe you."

"And I appreciate that," I interrupted. "I just loathe how Violet's suicide note wraps everything up."

He sighed. "It looks better this way. Especially in a snobby town like Spinderwood"

"I know."

Footsteps shuffled, making us crane our heads. Sadie stood in front of us with her hair bouncing around in the roaring wind.

She beamed her eyes. "Thank goodness you two fixed things."

Logan nodded. "I couldn't be happier."

"Me too," I said.

"Mind if I join you?" Sadie asked.

I gestured at her to sit down. "Of course not."

Sadie took her backpack off and shoved it on the table after sitting down.

Some people might have gotten annoyed by having a friend interrupt alone time with a boyfriend or girlfriend. But I wasn't that mean. Logan and I weren't up to anything private and didn't have to be left undisturbed. Besides, Sadie and I, being best friends, were a package deal. Kind of like how Grandma thought Gin and Tonic were a package deal. She should have been the mayor Gin and Tonic Town.

"How are things with Tony?" I asked.

She giggled. "Good. We're finally getting time to hangout because he's taking me to the movies tonight."

I nudged her shoulder. "A scary movie?"

Sadie rolled her eyes. "Please. You know how I feel

about those films."

***

The scent of chocolate wafted through the kitchen when I returned home, which meant Mom was baking. One quick glance at the oven confirmed I was right because it was on.

Damn. There was no way something bad could have happened. Life was too messy as it was. And I forgot to mention Logan was also with me in the kitchen. Yup. I took the risk of bringing Logan into the kitchen even if that meant running into family. I was a lot of things. But I had a good memory and remembered how Grandma used to lecture all the time about the importance of being a good host or hostess. And that meant letting Logan grab a snack or soda from the kitchen before we snooped through Grandma's bedroom.

Mom's eyes widened. "Company on a school night?"

"I'm helping Logan with his math homework," I said.

He nodded. "Yup."

"You're Logan?" Mom asked.

Logan chuckled. "Yes. Why?"

Mom picked her nail. "Casey has told me all about you."

I gave her a dirty look. "Mom!"

Good gracious. Mom needed to dial it back ASAP because she should have known how to act around company. Unless she aspired to be more like Grandma. Because Grandma would have been a little saucy if she ran into Logan and I right now.

She tucked a lock of her hair behind her ear. "I'm making brownies and could bring up a plate when they're done."

Logan bit his lip. "That's okay. I changed my mind about being hungry."

Thank goodness for Logan. I didn't need to give him

sort of secret signal that getting out of the kitchen ASAP was best. Life wasn't a spy movie, and I was supposed to be simplifying life.

"Wait, Casey," Mom said while Logan and I were about leave the kitchen.

We halted.

I titled my head back at Mom. "What is it?"

"I'm glad things are going well for you two. It's nice you have another friend outside of this house," she said.

I almost gritted my teeth. Sure. Mom hadn't said anything bad. But annoyance already fumed through my body a moment earlier. Logan and I needed to comb through Grandma's bedroom before everyone else got home. And having my family ask a million questions was what I needed. Please. Knowing I believed Violet didn't kill Grandma was the last thing my family needed to hear. I wasn't a jerk, and refused to make their lives more complicated until I had concrete proof.

Wait. Mom just referred to Logan as a friend. Maybe, just maybe, I shouldn't have blamed her. It wasn't like she had a problem with my sexuality and wanted to be mean. This was the same woman who would have given away all of her life savings just to avoid a fight. Like that time when she and Dad went out to dinner a few years. They had to wait for a table since the restaurant was crowded. Yet Mom convinced Dad to go to another restaurant after getting into an argument with another couple waiting in the restaurant's lobby.

I reached for his hand. "Logan is my boyfriend."

Her grin expanded. "My mistake."

"Don't worry about it. Anyway, let me know if you need any help with dinner later," I said.

Yup. I saved face despite how Logan and I weren't any closer to going through Grandma's bedroom. Having an opinion was one thing. But I didn't need to alienate Mom when too many dramatic things happened already.

"Will do." Mom turned her head to the oven after it

hummed.

But Logan and I didn't wait around for Mom to grab her oven mitts and take out the brownie tray. Nope. We would be in the kitchen till next Labor Day if we continued talking to her.

***

"That was more than a little awkward," Logan said after we entered Grandma's bedroom.

One look at Logan was all I needed to know he wasn't uptight like me. Another joke was all he needed to fall on the floor and burst into laughter. Because the muscles around his lips were so tight from suppressing his laughter. Yet I credited him for not showing his amusement. Some people might not have had the same willpower. Like me. I always struggled with whether laughing was or wasn't appropriate whenever Grandma told one of her stories. Like when she had three martinis and scallops one night out to dinner a couple of years. That evening was all fun and games until she got the bill. The Martinis ended up being twelve dollars a pop in addition to how the restaurant charge eighteen dollars for two emaciated scallops.

"I found something," he said. "It was behind the bedpost."

Great. I got preoccupied with my own thoughts and didn't notice how Logan kneeled on the floor and looked under Grandma's bed. Whatever. I should have been glad one of us was capable of not rambling and making a discovery—I wasn't stubborn enough to refuse help. I let Logan in on my theory and Violet's suicide being a farce for a reason. Unlike Grandma. She once made a comment about how she wouldn't turn to a Republican for help even if she was drowning.

Wait. The sparkle from the item Logan held should have caught my attention. Because it was just the type of thing Logan and I needed to find. Almost as if the universe threw us a bone.

"Do you know who the earring belongs to?" he asked.

I snorted. "It's not Grandma's."

"How do you know that?"

"She would never be caught dead with a green earring because she hated that color."

His jaw twitched. "Are you saying the earring belongs to the murderer?"

"Maybe."

CHAPTER 26

Theresa, Tony, Sadie, Logan, and I sat a table in the back of the lunch room the following day at school. And no. Liking the tables on the edge of the cafeteria didn't make me too controlling. It made me practical. Hearing what anyone had to say was next to impossible at the middle and front tables as a result of the collective chattering of various voices.

But I needed a minute of silence. Not everyone was lucky like me, and had people to sit with. There were always a few people that sat alone every single day. And I didn't even wanna imagine having a churning stomach from not fitting in. Wanting to be accepted and have friends was such a basic thing and shouldn't have been complicated. Yet it was. Or maybe I didn't want to think about my discovery yesterday afternoon. Because the earring as a step in the right direction, and I would find out who it belonged to ASAP.

Whatever. I could think about the earring later. Lunch would be over before I knew it, and one glance at my salad would have made Grandma scoff. She always believed in eating food while it was fresh.

Logan grinned. "How was the movie?"

"Fine." Sadie devoured the last bit of her tuna fish sandwich. "Although I'm gonna pick it next time."

Tony shrugged. "I didn't know the film would be violent."

Sadie snorted. "Sure. Let's go with that."

"I'm serious," Tony said.

"You could have read a review beforehand," I said.

Shit. I should have thought about my comment before speaking. It wasn't like I wanted to be rude, though. Looking at a review seemed to be the logical thing to do. Grandma always looked at what the critics said about a film before she even thought about seeing it. Something about not wasting her time, which seemed rather ironic for a woman had never once been on time in her life.

Tony sneered. "What's done is done."

"I'm glad I don't have to worry about a guy," Theresa said.

I lifted my eyebrows off my salad.

"I'm serious," Theresa continued. "Don't get me wrong. I don't think being in a relationship makes someone terrible. I'm just focused on fashion."

"Makes sense." Logan sipped some water.

"You should pursue your fashion more if you're serious about it," I said.

Theresa gave me the evil eye.

"I didn't mean anything bad by it." I had another bite of my salad before continuing. "I just meant you're talented, and need to start making things happen."

Theresa's eyes bugled. "And how should I do that?"

"Enter competitions, look for internships, and see if local boutique shops would sell your clothing on consignment," I suggested.

Theresa flipped her hair over her shoulders. "That's actually brilliant."

Being the bigger person meant ignoring how Theresa qualified her sentence with an adverb. Starting trouble was still the last thing I needed. Especially when the earring loomed in the back of my mind. Like when a mosquito kept buzzing in someone's face no matter how many times that person squatted it. Although I once again had to dwell on Grandma for a beat. Qualifying a statement was the type of thing Grandma did when she was alive. Such as when she mentioned not wanting to offend our family a couple of years ago when she implied someone in the family might have stolen her antique radio.

Logan winked at me. "I'm glad you're finally inviting me over to your beach this afternoon."

"You haven't invited Logan over yet?" Sadie munched on apple.

"I've been distracted," I said.

Tony gave me a mock frown. "That's the story of your life."

We all laughed. Yup. Even I could find something amusing about myself. Tony's words were true. I was more distracted than the white rabbit in the animated Disney *Alice and Wonderland* cartoon. Although I could at least be thankful I didn't have a watch that was two days late. Because that would have defied logic.

***

Logan and I sat on two lounge chairs on the beach after school while the salt water scent trickled through the air as the scorching sand pressed against my feet. Although the humid sand wasn't a bad thing. It wasn't like someone surrounded me with fire. I just wanted to enjoy every last minute of warmth before fall and winter arrived. Even if Grandma would have made some comment about how it was already too cold. Because she was always cold. Like that time several weeks before her death when it was 80 something degrees and she still insisted on making a fire in the living room.

"We need to decide what we're gonna do with the earring." He put his sunglasses on. Yup. I wasn't the only one who left them clipped to my shirt and not on my head.

"I don't wanna go to the police."

Logan scoffed. "I didn't say we should."

He needed to relax ASAP. I just didn't trust the police in Spinderwood after how they handled Grandma's murder investigation with being more concerned about taking the easy way out than getting justice.

"We still have nothing to go on," I said.

Yup. I had to be the guy who played devil's advocate. We needed to find the clue that would unravel Grandma's murder. Finding the ultimate clue was the million-dollar question, though. Because it might as well have existed in thin air.

He exhaled a long breath. "You need to be patient."

"I don't need a lecture."

"I wasn't trying to lecture you. It's just a fact."

I remained silent since I needed to choose my next words carefully. Saying the wrong thing wasn't on today's agenda.

"Why don't you put sunscreen on my back." Logan tossed me the bottle.

Wait. I didn't mention how Logan was shirtless. Because I appreciated a hot person as much as the next individual. A beach was one of the few places where a guy could be shirtless without raising alarm. We were also on private property, which was the same argument Grandma used when Uncle Brad caught her topless sunbathing a couple of summers ago. The incident was so awkward that Uncle Brad and Grandma didn't speak to each other for a month after it happened.

"What are you waiting for?" he asked.

Wow. Logan sat down on my knee already.

I opened the bottle, and squirted sunscreen onto his back. I leaned my head, letting my lips touch his neck.

Every cell in my body became electrified while my heart fluttered faster. Damn. Rubbing the sunscreen in good shouldn't have been this erotic. Hold on. I shouldn't have used the word erotic. I just kissed him, as opposed to having sex on the lounge chair. Although I would soak up every last second of this moment. It would be fleeting like everything else in life. And that meant not having any qualms about rubbing in the sunscreen slower. Besides, I wasn't still kissing him. I was now focused on my skin touching his. Kind of like that time when my family took a trip to Barbados and Grandma had a hot local rub sunscreen on her despite Dad's skepticism.

Someone kicked up sand.

"Hi, Poppy," I said, removing my hands from Logan's back.

She giggled. "Don't stop on my account."

"I was rubbing in some sunscreen," I said.

"You can never be too careful. At least according to my mom," Logan said.

Poppy unfolded a lounge chair and set it up next to me. "It's sweet you two have each other."

I smiled. "Thanks."

Poppy didn't respond. Instead, she remained silent.

My gaze shifted to the flute in her right hand. "Hard day at work?"

She twirled a strand of hair with a free finger. "Yes. But Brad was nice enough to let me out early."

"Nice to meet you, Poppy," Logan said.

She shipped some of her Champagne. "That's right. I don't think we've met before."

"Where are my manners? I should have introduced you two," I said, laughing.

"There's no need for formalities, Casey." Poppy chugged her remaining Champagne.

Logan glanced at Poppy. "What do you think about Violet's suicide?"

Having faith in Logan meant not giving him a dirty

look. There was a difference between mentioning Grandma's murder with Aunt Rita, Uncle Brad, Mom, Dad, and a teenager, or cool adult. Getting another perspective on the situation could be beneficial. Logan and I could only think about Grandma's death for so long before our heads exploded.

"Some people get what's coming to them," Poppy said.

Damn. I never once thought Poppy was cruel. Although I shouldn't have been too critical of her. She claimed a couple of reporters accosted her after the news about Grandma giving Violet for adoption as a teen leaked to the press. Because I didn't care how much money someone paid me. I wouldn't have traded places with Poppy since dealing with rowdy reporters just wasn't appealing. Nothing in the constitution said I had to cooperate with them.

"That's a little harsh," Logan said.

Okay. Maybe he had more guts than I realized. A response could provoke Poppy even more. I wasn't oblivious to her raised voice when she made that jab at Violet.

Her lips curled. "Not really. Grandma didn't deserve to die."

"I didn't say that," Logan replied.

Poppy gasped. "What are you saying?"

"A suicide is an easy way to wrap up a murder," Logan said.

Look at him go. He refused to back down. And a part of me even loved him for his tenacity. Everyone needed to draw a line in the sand at some point. Like when Grandma told me a story about one of her friends ending a friendship over going through six rolls of toilet paper in one week and clogging the toilet.

She gripped her glass tighter. "The simplest explanations are sometimes the right ones."

"I suppose," he said.

Poppy fidgeted in the lounge chair. "What do you

think, Casey?"

"I agree with Logan. Someone is blowing a lot of smoke," I said.

"Whatever. I need to get more Champagne." Poppy stood.

Logan chuckled. "Just because the police can't solve the murder doesn't mean Casey and I can't play detectives?"

She held her glass tighter. "You're actually looking into things?"

A seagull's screech echoe through the air before landing a few yards away from me. It lowered its head, and nibbled on something in the sand. Although I wouldn't have a mediation about how life would have been simpler if I were a seagull. Poppy's agitation was my biggest priority right now.

"Yup," Logan responded.

"I'm just so sick of this bullshit. Everyone keeps talking about Grandma's murder and Violet all over town. It's not like there isn't more to gossip about in Spinderwood." Poppy screamed, and the Champagne flute fell onto the sand before breaking into a bunch of shards. Wow. Perhaps she was stressed about more than work. Being pissed off was one thing, but the rage flashing through Poppy's eyes was another. "Fuck."

I exhaled a breath. "Logan and I will clean up the glass."

She grinned. "Thanks."

Poppy left without another word before I blinked. Although she once again kicked up more sand as she walked away while huffing.

"Some people can be so touchy," Logan said.

Poppy had worked for Uncle Brad for a fair amount of time, which meant tasks shouldn't have surprised her. Yet I wouldn't forget her unhinged behavior. Temporary annoyance was one thing. Like in the kitchen when I walked in on Poppy's conversation with Uncle Brad. But

Poppy's demeanor moments earlier told a different story. It was a side of Poppy that I never saw before.

CHAPTER 27

My life might as well have been a Tim Burton movie. I just had to point out the obvious about how something creepy existed from being in Grandma's study several days after my conversation with Poppy. Although life wasn't completely terrible. Logan was with me too, which meant I had someone to share the guilt with about wanting to check Grandma's emails. Like that time when Grandma was stuck in an elevator for five hours, but was comforted because Grandpa was with her.

"I still think the police should have checked her email," I said, getting comfortable in the chair while Logan and I sat in front of Grandma's desk, waiting for the laptop to load.

"You don't have to say that again. Although we can't get too mad at the police. This isn't television show where they can chase every little red herring," Logan said.

"I know." I rested a hand under my chin. Yup. Grandma's laptop was such a piece of shit that it took at least several minutes before arriving at the home screen. I was even a little embarrassed for Uncle Brad. He gave Grandma this laptop a few years ago after buying a new one for himself.

I wasn't being harsh, though. I never told Uncle Brad what I thought about his behavior since I kept my opinion to myself. Giving someone a ten-year-old laptop was like giving someone a used condom.

Logan jabbed my shoulder. "Get going."

I opened Safari, and went onto Gmail before logging into Grandma's email. Wow. I never once thought Grandma asking me technology questions would benefit me. But it had. Sure. There was no guarantee Logan and I would find anything incriminating on her email. Yet we had to look. Satisfying our curiosity would allow us to move onto the next theory.

"Did you find anything?" Logan asked.

"Give me a moment." I continued scrolling through her inbox.

"No problem."

"Bingo." I looked up at him.

"What is it?" he asked.

I coughed, clearing the nervousness from my throat. Goosebumps also remained glued to my arms and back even though dwelling on the fear jolting my body wasn't best. Grandma should have been alive, and we all should have been having a nice afternoon. But no. The universe had other plans.

"Well?" Logan demanded.

"She got an email from Savyguru@gmail.com three days before she died," I revealed.

His eyebrows inched up. "And we should care about a correspondence from a silly email address because?"

"It's not what the person wrote. It's how the person said it," I said. "The person threatened to come for Grandma if she exposed her secret."

Logan took out his iPhone.

"Do you really need to be using your phone right

now?" I asked.

He laughed. "It's not what you think."

Logan opened an app before his iPhone made a clicking sound. Figures. I was too preoccupied with the email to realize taking a photo of it was a good idea. The truth was I didn't know what I was doing. And that meant assuming the guilty person could hack into Grandma's email and delete the email.

The doorknob turned, making my pulse echo in my ear while I closed the laptop lid. Mom now stood at the room's entrance, and my breathing could slow down. My current situation was not as awkward as when Grandma was five seconds away from catching Tony masturbating last summer. Although why Tony told me that story remained a mystery. Nothing good came from me knowing that tale.

"Why did you have the door closed?" Mom asked.

Good question. Being put on the spot and lying was the best thing ever. Doing so was such a useful skill because it would ensure I got into the CIA.

"And why were you on your grandma's laptop?" Mom demanded, folding her arms.

"He was showing me a slideshow of his trip to Paris he took with his grandma last summer, and got emotional," Logan interrupted. "I thought it'd be good to shut the door and give him privacy."

Her mouth gaped. "Oh."

Damn. Logan deserved to win the best boyfriend of the year award. Even I wouldn't have been able to lie on the spot like he just did. Whatever. I was just glad I told him about my trip to Paris because I didn't know how we would have lied our way out of the situation otherwise.

I sneered. "What do you want?"

"To see if you'd like cookies," Mom said.

"You baked again?" I asked.

"It helps me deal with the stress of garden club," Mom said.

I shook my head. "You should quit if you don't like the club."

Mom clutched her pearl necklace. "I like the club. I just don't like the bureaucracy part."

***

"I wanted to apologize, Casey," Mom said hours later.

We were in the kitchen having milk and cookies. Aunt Rita, Poppy, Uncle Brad, and Dad had gone for a ride in Uncle Brad's boat while Mom and I stayed behind. Yup. I had to be the guy who thought Uncle Brad was a pretentious jerk.

Uncle Brad and Aunt Rita loved their damned boat too much because they always went out for a ride every chance they got. But they didn't need to rub it in everyone's face. Almost like Uncle Brad overcompensated for not being well endowed. I had been so flabbergasted with how Grandma was always impressed when Uncle Brad and Aunt Rita took her or her and the family out for a boat ride. Almost like they walked on water. Although Uncle Brad and Aunt Rita had never been able to turn water into gin or wine for Grandma.

Hold on. Mom wanted to apologize, which meant listening for once in my life. Adults didn't often express contrition when dealing with teenagers.

"I shouldn't have embarrassed you in front of Logan," she continued. "It's not like you were watching porn and thinking about having sex."

I glared at her. "Mom!"

"I'm not gonna apologize for being honest. I know teenagers think about sex."

Good gracious. I so wanted to have a sex talk with Mom. I stayed up all night every night hoping to have flushed cheeks while Mom talked to me about sex.

"Anyway, I'm just glad you aren't impressed with

123

Uncle Brad's boat either," I added.

"I'm just pleased you're happy. You deserve to have something positive to focus on."

"Thanks." I ate another cookie. The mixture of the doughy, buttery, sugary, and vanilla flavors jolted my taste buds. Damn. There was nothing like the comfort of a sugar cookie since they provided short-term comfort despite how Grandma believed they were the devil's invention. Something about how the devil wanted her to gain weight and God wanted her to resist gluttony. I usually tuned Grandma out when it came to her dieting talk. She had always been on a diet, but was never successful. Even though she had been dieting since Nixon.

She finished her milk. "We should have Logan over for dinner one night. I wouldn't even have to cook. We could order Chinese food."

"That'd be nice."

Sure. I could have mentioned how having Logan over for dinner might be awkward. But the scorching sensation jabbing my stomach from having my boyfriend meet my family wasn't completely terrible. It meant having life return to some semblance of normalcy. Rambling also meant procrastinating. Not thinking about the earring under Grandma's bed and Poppy's possible sketchy behavior was easier than contemplating what the hell happened to Grandma and Violet.

CHAPTER 28

Intruding in someone's bedroom wasn't kind, but I had a good a reason to invade Poppy's privacy the following afternoon. And it wasn't because of her tense behavior such as dropping the Champagne flute on the beach. Nope. My reasoning was simpler than that. Mom asked me to return Poppy's laundry basket, containing cleaned clothes since she had to take a phone call.

Anyway, my point was that was why I was in her room when a ripped envelope sticking out from a pile of books on Poppy's desk caught my attention.

Wait. Returning Poppy's laundry was one thing, but I shouldn't have snooped. I would have been the first person to get pissed off if someone invaded my privacy. Like that time Dad got the mail because a package arrived from him, yet Grandma was paranoid because of being afraid Dad would open her credit card bill and find out how much she owed American Express.

There would be plenty of time for contrition later, though. I just couldn't ignore the ripped envelope.

I walked over to her and desk and grabbed the envelop in question. Doing so scattered the pile of books and made half fall to the floor. But I was too concerned with the letter's contents to pick up the books even if smart people covered their tracks.

Good gracious. So much for Grandma's murder and Violet's "suicide" being the latest scandalous events in Spinderwood. The letter was from Poppy's college and was dated from last January. But those were just minor details compared to how Poppy was kicked out of school for failing all her classes that semester.

Wow. And I thought Logan was a good liar when Mom walked into Grandma's study on while Logan and I played detective. But he had nothing on Poppy. How she tricked the whole family on how she wanted to take a leave of absence was beyond me. Then again, it made more sense than I cared to admit. And my opinion had nothing to do with thinking I was psychic and reading Poppy's mind. I leave that sort of thing in the past where it belonged. Yup. Grandma used to visit her psychic all the time. Like when she frequented her psychic a lot the second year after Grandpa died. Her psychic kept telling Grandma she would meet a rich man. Yet she never did. Anyway, the point was, Poppy started working for Uncle Brad a couple of weeks after the letter was sent, which was easy cover. Nobody would suspect her of hiding something if she gained real world experiencing by helping Uncle Brad with the publishing company's accounting.

The door creaked. Yet I continued staring at the letter even though the hairs on my back should have been pricked. A serial killer could have walked into the room with a chain saw and I still would haven't budged.

"What the hell are you doing?" Poppy asked.

I spun around. "I didn't mean to read the letter."

"Didn't ask for an apology."

Way to be direct. I so needed to feel worse than I already did for being somewhere I didn't belong. Like when

Grandpa criticized Grandma for spending twenty thousand dollars on bushes because she didn't want to deal with a neighbor.

"You didn't answer my question," Poppy spat.

"I was returning your laundry."

Her eyes drifted to the letter, which I held tighter. She then looked at the floor in front of her desk where the books were before moving her focus to the desk. But she walked towards the door before closing it instead of screaming or yelling. And it wasn't long until tears dripped down her face. Apparently, Grandma didn't have a monopoly on being theatrical.

Poppy clenched a fist. "You can't tell anyone."

I sighed. "I wasn't planning on it."

"You have no idea how much pressure I was under that semester between dealing with lousy professors and my breakup with Derek."

"I understand."

Shit. I shouldn't have pretended to know what Poppy felt. I wasn't her. Because I would have the first person to have rage fuming through my body if someone said they knew how I felt.

Wait. The threatening email Grandma received mentioned a secret. Perhaps Grandma found out Poppy flunked out of school and threatened to tell Aunt Rita unless Poppy came clean. Nah. Poppy couldn't have killed Grandma. I did what I always did and jumped to conclusion because that was easier than dealing with the reality of Poppy's academic issue and Grandma's murder being two separate issues.

She grabbed my hand. "Please don't tell my mother. You have no idea how tough she is."

"I know how to keep a secret."

Sure. I had never been involved in terrible situations, but Grandma mentioned numerous incriminating stories to me over the years. Yet I hadn't slipped by telling anyone Mom, Dad, or Logan.

She gave me a devilish smile. "Thank you."

"And I really am sorry."

Yup. I had to over apologize Expressing regret once wasn't enough, and I needed to become redundant.

"Don't worry about it." She rubbed both of her eyes.

***

I tapped Logan's back the following morning at school. He turned his body to face me.

"You'll never believe what I discovered yesterday," I said.

Sure. I emphasized being able to keep a secret with Poppy yesterday. And I sort of stood by my promise because I had no reason to snitch and tell Aunt Rita the truth. But Logan was my boyfriend, which meant he was the one person I was allowed to tell secrets too. Like how Grandma revealed to me how she used to tell Grandpa her real opinion about people. Logan was also my partner in crime with investigating Grandma's murder, which was reason enough to confide in him.

His eyes lit up. "Did you find out who killed your grandma?"

"Nope. It's juicier."

He put another textbook in his backpack. "You can't be serious."

"I am."

"What is it?"

"Poppy flunked out of school last fall, which is probably why she started working for Uncle Brad."

He zipped up his backpack. "Interesting."

"I hope you don't think I'm a terrible person for gossiping."

"Don't be ridiculous. You're only human," Logan said.

I raised my eyebrows. "What's that supposed to mean?"

"Nothing. I just meant I would do the same thing if I were in your position."

Good to know Logan and I had a similar thought process. Thinking he was a better person than because he wouldn't gossip would have made my skin crawl. But I got ahead of myself since there was no need to invent a problem that didn't exist. Like when Grandma screamed for 20 minutes last winter when the weather forecast predicted a three-foot blizzard. The storm never came, and Grandma's theatrics had therefore been for nothing.

Logan grimaced. "Wait. You don't think Poppy killed your grandma because she uncovered what happened?"

I shook my head in a vigorous fashion. "I already considered that possibility."

"And?"

"She doesn't have it in her to kill someone. Just look how she reacted on the beach that day."

He winked. "You certainly enjoyed putting sunscreen on me."

I nudged him. "You should be flattered I think you're so hot."

"I am."

"You can't tell anyone about what I told you," I said.

He closed his locker, making it clink. "I won't."

"What can't you tell anyone?" asked someone.

Sadie, Tony, and Theresa stood to the right of us. Great. Just what we needed. Telling Logan was one thing. But I had no desire to reveal Poppy's secret to anyone else. Tony and Theresa were family lived in the same house as Aunt Rita, which meant numerous opportunities to slip up and blab Poppy's secret. And it wasn't even that trust was an issue. It wasn't. Tony and Theresa proved they were reliable by hanging out with me over the summer when Sadie was gone. But I still couldn't take a risk. A little booze was all Tony or Theresa needed to slip up.

"Nothing," Logan said.

Sadie crossed her arms. "Tell us what you were talking about."

"It doesn't matter," I said.

Tony huffed. "No use in trying to change his mind. I know a moot point when I see one."

Sadie ran her fingers through her hair. "Fair enough."

"Couples are also supposed to keep secrets," Tony added.

"Agreed. But I'm more stressed about all the homework I've gotten since the start of the school year," Sadie said.

I snickered. "The quarter is only halfway done."

"I know, and that's the worst part," Sadie said.

CHAPTER 29

Sunlight poked through my curtains the following morning, then I rubbed my eyes and yawned. I got out of bed and walked towards my desk. Reading Violet's letter to Grandma seemed logical. Sure. Discovering a new clue or getting a fresh perspective wasn't guaranteed. But I could try since I had nothing to lose.

There was only one problem, though. The letter was gone. I hadn't moved it since keeping under my desk planner. Come to think of it, I couldn't remember the last time I saw the letter. Not that I needed to pinpoint an exact date the letter vanished—I needed to be more concerned with it being stolen.

My back hairs stood up. Lacking concrete proof wasn't mutually exclusive with worrying. I might not have known what happened to the letter, but someone took it. That much was sure. Stealing was the only explanation I could think of. It wasn't like the note would fly away. Nope. Life still wasn't some Disney cartoon.

Hold on. I was being too general by failing to appreciate the bigger picture. Taking the letter meant someone was in my room. And thievery meant Grandma's and Violet's deaths were more complicated than the Spinderwood police realized, and my hunch about the killer still being out there had to be correct. Yet I wasn't any closer to discovering who killed Grandma and staged Violet's death as a suicide…

***

The scent of coffee filled the air when I stepped into the kitchen. Great. Poppy was only the person in the kitchen, which meant she made the coffee. And I so wanted her to make the coffee. I loved the coffee the previous time she made it and spent every single night praying she would make it again.

She smiled. "I made coffee."

"Thanks, but I'll just stick to milk and cereal."

"Whatever."

"Damn. Everything takes too fucking long." Her eyes moved back to the coffee machine. Coffee was still in the process of dripping into the pot. In fact, it wasn't even at the halfway point.

"No need to panic." I finished pouring the milk into my bowl and took a spoonful of the Honey nut Cheerios.

Her nostrils flared. "Easy for you to say."

"Did I do something wrong?"

"Other than sneaking into my room?"

I remained silent. Doing so was best. Letting Poppy speak her mind was easier than facing an argument I didn't have time for.

She sighed. "Sorry about my mood."

"Would it help to discuss it?"

She hung her head lower. "I lost one of my earrings the night Grandma died and haven't been able to find it."

Funny someone else should lose something in the mansion. First someone took Uncle Brad's gun, and then

132

someone took Violet's letter from me, and now a third event. Almost like there was a thief living among us.

Okay. Fine. Thief was a weak word. Grandma and Violet were dead, which meant this situation was a double homicide. And I would stick to my theory about Violet being murdered. Being consistent was also a good thing because it showed I wasn't impulsive.

"What color are they?" I asked.

"Green, and they look shiny and sparkly in direct sunlight."

Jumping to assumptions wasn't kind, but Poppy gave me a concrete clue whether she knew it or not. The earring Logan found under the bed was green. Although I was smarter about the earring than I was about Violet's letter. The earring was tucked away in my boxer drawer because that seemed to be the last place someone would go snooping through my stuff.

Getting sidetracked was the last thing I needed to do right now, though. There was a good chance the earring could have been Poppy's. Yet the possible discovery was still an enigma. I didn't have any concrete proof of Poppy doing anything and understood how accusing her of something without any certainty would only cause tension.

Poppy elevated her eyebrows. "Something wrong?"

"I just have a lot of school work."

She giggled. "Lighten up. You're only young once."

"I know."

"I could speak to your parents if they're giving you stress. My teen years weren't that long ago."

"Thanks, but I'm good."

My pulse hammered in my ears. No. I had to be wrong. Poppy couldn't be capable of killing anyone. There just had to be a good explanation for my discovery. I knew it. Like that time Grandma wanted to believe there was a good explanation for someone drinking all of her gin. Apparently, there was a discrepancy between what she drank and what she saw in the bottle the following afternoon.

Footsteps squeaked against the floor. Great. Mom walked into the kitchen, and happened to have a glare on her face. And I so wanted her to give me a lecture.

"You should have left for school ten minutes ago," Mom said.

Poppy rolled her eyes. "Don't blame, Casey. I've been chatting him up."

"I don't care what the reason is for him getting side-tracked. He needs to get a move on," Mom said.

Mom needed a shot of hard liquor ASAP. I wasn't a delinquent; I was just a little preoccupied. It wasn't like I robbed a bank or killed someone.

***

Telling Logan my concern about Poppy and Violet's missing letter wouldn't be easy. But it had to be done. And maybe, just maybe, I needed to be optimistic. At least for a moment. Sharing the latest update with Logan meant I had someone to talk to and wouldn't have to suffer alone.

Suffer was the wrong word, though. Nothing bad happened. Yet I might as well have been suffering. My cousin couldn't be a murder. Nope. I refused to believe I was living with a murderer. That meant Poppy could just walk into my bedroom and slit my throat in the middle of the night.

Enough. Logan walked into the hallway and I needed to get his attention ASAP. My grumbling stomach wasn't for nothing, and that meant wanting to eat. But no. I had to do the right thing and talk to Logan. He offered to be my "partner" in all of this.

Logan glanced at me. "Hi, Casey."

"We need to talk."

"Okay."

The bell rang, meaning our lunch period officially started. There also happened to be a few kids scurrying by. But I didn't have time to wonder if the students were in a hurry because they were hungry like I was or because they had a class to go to.

"I think the earring we found under Grandma's bed belongs to Poppy," I said before taking a minute to pause and continued with what Poppy told me.

"Interesting," Logan said after a beat.

I flinched. "What do you think?"

I just had to be direct and not dance around the issue. Equivocation would only make life more complicated. Like when Dad used to grill Grandma about how many days a week she had a martini after coming from work.

"The truth?" Logan asked.

"I would expect nothing less."

"I don't know what to think."

No. My question wasn't mean to be some open-ended English essay. Logan needed to give me a concrete answer like yesterday.

"If Poppy really did kill your grandma, then we need to keep your suspicion to ourselves. At least until we gather more evidence," Logan said.

Yup. I couldn't argue with Logan since I didn't know much about Grandma's and Violet's deaths.

He squeezed my hand. "You aren't scared of Poppy, are you?"

Great. It was my turn to answer a loaded question. Like when Grandma asked me a year ago if I started studying for the SAT's. Apparently, it was never too early to start thinking about my future. Because Grandma only wanted the best for me when was alive.

"Not at the moment," I said.

He sucked in a breath. "I live across the street. And you have Sadie too."

"Perhaps we should take up my mom on her suggestion."

"What are you talking about?" Logan asked.

"She made a remark about inviting you over for a meet and greet."

Logan rubbed his forehead. "Hmmm. Maybe that would be a good way to get a read on Poppy."

And all was right with the world. For the moment, that was. Because I should have realized Logan would put my mind at ease.

Yup. Informing Logan about my concerns was the right thing to do. Spending time with Poppy at a family dinner was an easy way to get to know her without arousing suspicious.

CHAPTER 30

"Thank you so much for having me over," Logan said the following evening.

Mom, Dad, Theresa, Tony, Poppy, Aunt Rita, Uncle Brad, Logan, and I sat at the dining room table. There was a plate, wine glass, and napkin with a fork, knife, and spoon in front of everyone. Several wine bottles were at each end of the table. And there was no doubt Grandma would have approved of the presentation. Because she lived and died for decorum. I even once asked her if she hoped the Queen of England would stop by. She then responded by what was wrong with hoping to see Queen Elizabeth before stomping out of the room. The tablecloth also deserved praise by having several flamingos etched on it. Call me crazy. There was just something unique about choosing birds that weren't native to Connecticut for a tablecloth design. But the two candles with flames flickering from them put the final touch on tonight's festivities.

Yup. Mom lit the dining room candles for atmosphere

even though this wasn't the fourteenth century, and we had electricity. But I needed to save my internal rambling for later since Logan and I got what we wanted, and could observe Poppy.

"No need for formalities," Mom said before pouring herself a more than generous serving of white wine.

Dad looked at Logan's wine glass. "Maybe we should have stuck with sparkling cider. We wouldn't want to overstep."

"I had Champagne at the birthday party," Logan said.

A silence swept over the room.

Blaming Logan for mentioning Grandma would have been unfair. He didn't strike me as a mean person. What he said was the truth since he enjoyed Champagne at Grandma's 60th birthday.

Poppy snorted. "Lighten up. He doesn't have far to get home."

Dad scratched his chin. "That's true."

"Besides, it's a professional development day tomorrow, which means no school," Mom added.

"Shit. I forgot we had the day off," Tony said, scooping some rice onto his plate one of the takeout cartons.

Aunt Rita glared at Tony. Although I wouldn't ramble about her being a prude and afraid of cursing. And I could pretend to feel normal for a second by enjoying having my boyfriend over for dinner. It also wasn't my problem that Aunt Rita needed to get a grip. There were worse things in life than cursing. Like that time Grandma's bad day became worse by a bird crapping on her fur coat.

"It's so nice Casey has a boyfriend." Mom broke off a bit of her dumpling and dunked it in sauce before devouring it in a matter of seconds.

Okay. Fine. Maybe Aunt Rita wasn't the only one who would glare tonight. Having Logan for dinner might have been great, but Mom didn't need to make me blush. Red cheeks were one thing worth eliminating because I didn't crave the spotlight like Grandma had when she was alive.

Mom bit her lip. "Sorry. I didn't mean anything bad by it, Casey."

Dad turned to Mom. "Maybe I worried about the wrong person."

Mom pursed her lips.

"I'm kidding," Dad said.

Uncle Brad looked at Logan. "It was so nice having you at the company this summer. You were Rose's favorite intern."

"You don't have to flatter me," Logan said.

"It's the truth. She told me herself." Uncle Brad chugged some of his red wine.

Frowning at Uncle Brad for drinking a boring wine would have happened any other night. But I could pretend to be carefree tonight. The real focus should have been on Logan getting a read on Poppy.

Poppy twirled a strand of her hair. "No harm in accepting a free compliment."

Bingo. Poppy said something. The only problem was that she hadn't said anything damning.

Logan cracked a smile. "Agreed."

"I love it when people compliment me on my fashion." Theresa poured herself more wine.

"And how is that going?" Poppy asked.

"Not fast enough," Theresa said.

Mom patted Theresa's hand. "Give it time."

"I'm sure you're right," Theresa replied.

I stuck my fork into a piece of chicken before shoving into my mouth. A mixture of spicy, tangy, and sweet flavors lit up every cell in my mouth. Yup. I had to describe General Tsao's Chicken. It was my favorite Chinese food dish, which made tonight's dinner with Logan even more epic. Chinese food also made nostalgia jolt my mind. Grandma used to take me out for Chinese food all the time. And there was nothing funnier than Grandma at a

Chinese restaurant because she could never make up her mind about what to order.

Dad grabbed the napkin in front of him, and wiped his mouth. "It's interesting you took the internship, Logan."

I grunted. "Not this again."

"What is your dad getting at?" Logan asked.

Dad beamed his eyes. "I'm not trying to criticize you, Casey. I just think you should have interned with the company. She would have loved to have you intern with her."

"There's nothing wrong with forging my own path," I said.

"Casey's right," Poppy said. "Taking the easy way doesn't build character."

Interesting. Poppy once again said something nice. Because her kindness had two possible interpretations. She could have been genuine and wanted to keep the peace. Or she could have been putting on a façade.

Okay. Confession time. Mine and Logan's plan wasn't perfect. Getting a good read on someone in one evening wasn't realistic. Knowing whether someone was good or bad took time, and couldn't be rushed.

"I think he was being stubborn," Dad said.

"I agree with Poppy," Aunt Rita said.

"I'm all for the easy way." Uncle Brad swirled the contents of his glass before giving it a good sniff and sipping it.

Aunt Rita sneered. "You would say that."

Wow. Not knowing any better would have entailed making a comment about tension in Uncle Brad and Aunt Rita's marriage. But I knew better. I was seventeen; not a child. Starting a possible argument after everyone had been drinking also didn't seem smart. Our family hadn't had enough shit happen and so needed to be dragged through the mud even more.

"At least Casey made a bunch of short story submissions to literary magazines," Mom said.

No shock pulsed through my body from Mom's comment—she must not have wanted a fight. It wasn't like she could go ten rounds with someone in a verbal argument. Nope. The other person would have decimated her, and that wouldn't have been a pretty sight. Like Grandma's previously mentioned fur coat, which got pooped on.

***

I walked into the kitchen hours later to look for my iPhone. Uncle Brad happened to be drinking scotch, and I almost screamed. It just seemed a little odd for him to be standing in the dark. Like he wanted to reenact a bad horror movie or something.

He craned his head. "It was nice to meet Logan."

"Thanks." I grabbed my iPhone from the counter.

Phew. The crisis was over. I didn't know what I would have done if my iPhone wasn't in the kitchen. Losing one more thing would have been tragedy. And maybe, just maybe, our family would make the news for all the things our family had misplaced. Yup. The list was ever growing. I would forget about Poppy's earring, Uncle Brad's gun, or Violet's letter no matter how hard I tried.

"I didn't mean to interrupt your thinking," I continued.

He chugged the rest of his glass before pouring himself a refill from the half empty scotch bottle on the counter. "Don't worry about it. I could use someone to talk to."

"What do you mean?"

He pouted. "I should go to bed…"

No way Uncle Brad could go to bed. He was the one who piqued my curiosity, which meant it was only fair for him to finish his point. Like when one of Grandma's soap operas teased a possible hookup, only to not follow through. There was nothing like a disappointing plot point to make Grandma knock over a vase. And I wasn't joking.

Grandma once threw a plate across the room after being unhappy with one of the storylines on *Days of our Lives*.

"I have discretion," I said.

"I didn't want to think the worst of her."

"I'm not following."

"Poppy had me lie for her the night of the sixtieth birthday party."

I scowled. "You're going to have to be more specific."

"She wasn't with me because of needing to sober up."

"Where was she?" I demanded.

His shoulders bounced up. "I don't know. But I wish I did."

"You don't think Poppy killed Grandma, do you?"

"I'm not sure what to think anymore." Uncle Bard collapsed onto the kitchen counter before snoring.

Whatever. Uncle Brad was safe at home and couldn't make a fool of himself by getting into more trouble. Like that time when Grandma went out clubbing and a photo of Dad and Mom walking her to the car while her cheeks were flushed and she sported a "happy" smile somehow made it onto *TMZ*.

Yeah. I would find a good explanation regardless of whether some people might have chastised me for making excuses for Poppy. I couldn't help myself, though. Admitting I lived with a possible murderer just didn't roll off my tongue no matter how many times I tried wrapping my head around the issue.

***

"Thanks for meeting me," I said a few minutes later after shutting the front door and sitting on the top step.

"You're lucky I find you adorable," Logan said.

I exhaled a breath. "Yes. I know it's late."

"What's so important?"

"We have more reason to be suspicious about Poppy."

The wind whistled, making a branch snap and fall to the ground. An owl also hooted from another tree as the stars and moon glowed in the night sky. But now wasn't the time to think about a serial killer lurking nearby and all the other horrors associated with nighttime. I had to get to the point since I would have been the first to criticize anyone else for wasting time.

Logan nodded. "I'm listening."

I wasn't making things any easier by not being direct. But I couldn't admit the truth to Logan. Being honest meant saying the problem out loud, and I couldn't be 100 percent sure if that was a step I was ready for. Yet. I texted Logan in the middle of the night and needed to own that fact. And that meant not wasting Logan's time. Because I respected him enough to not jerk him around.

"My Uncle Brad gave Poppy a phony alibi," I said.

His jaw shook. "You have to be joking."

"I'm not."

"What are we supposed to do now?"

"We know where Poppy lives…"

CHAPTER 31

O nce again going into Poppy's room the following morning wasn't smart. Getting her mad by making it obvious someone went into her room would have been wrong if Poppy was the killer. But I didn't have a choice in light of Uncle Brad's revelation from last night. Today was also the perfect time to snoop. Poppy would be at work with Uncle Brad, and I needed to make use of having my professional development day off. Having Logan here helped too. His presence meant I wasn't alone. Although now was no time to think about Grandma's favorite corny expression about icing on the cake.

"Are you nervous?" Logan asked.

"Do you even have to ask?"

I smiled. Poppy's laptop was on her desk as I anticipated. Everyone in Grandma's publishing company always did work business on the company computers, not personal computers.

Her laptop being left behind was only one step of the process. I still wasn't sure if she had a password for her login page or if she logged out of email every single time. But there was no harm in following my hunch. Especially if it ruled out Poppy's email being the one that sent the nasty email to Grandma.

Turning on her laptop didn't make me frown. She didn't have a password to get to the homepage. Although she did log out of her email every single time because clicking the Gmail part on her tab prompted needing a password. But all hope wasn't lost. Gmail gave her email, which was savyguru@gmail.com.

"Shit," Logan said.

I turned to him. "Don't be so harsh. We know Poppy sent the email to my grandma."

"But we still need proof."

There was no guarantee my latest hunch would be correct, but I had to try. It wasn't like I could die from seeing if my guess was correct.

"Bingo," I said after typing the password and shifting in the chair to get more comfortable.

Damn. If only Poppy had a wheelie chair. Having that type of chair was preferable over her stiff red oak chair.

"I'm impressed." Logan gave me a quick kiss.

"Let's just be glad I remembered *Grey's Anatomy* is her favorite show."

He snickered. "But why would that be her password?"

"Don't know, don't care."

Wow. Poppy actually did it. I had proof she sent the email to Grandma since the message was still in her send folder. Because I so wanted someone to burst into the room and yell surprise before rambling about my cousin possibly being a murderer.

I pushed the laptop towards Logan. "See the truth for yourself."

"What do we do?" Logan asked after looking at the email.

"We still don't have proof she killed Grandma."

He pouted. "What more proof do we need? We know her earring was under your Grandma's bed in addition to how your Uncle Brad lied to her. And it doesn't help that Violet's letter is missing. Maybe she stole that so she could forge the suicide note."

"That's a big if."

"Why are you waffling?" he asked.

Great question. I woke up every morning wanting to act weak. Please. As if anyone with one ounce of common sense should have understood my hesitation. Poppy was my cousin.

He looped his arm around me. "I'm sorry. This must be difficult for you as it is, and I shouldn't make it more challenging."

A crueler person would have responded with a petty remark. But that wasn't fair. Logan tried being nice to me by apologizing for his comment, and I needed to show him the same respect.

"No worries," I said.

"But there's no harm in not doing anything until we have proof."

Maybe things weren't as dire with Logan as I thought. Not rushing to do something showed Logan was capable of restraining himself. And that was a good thing. Acting based off emotion was never good. Dangerous situations required thoughtful, precise responses. Making the Grandma-Violet with Poppy maybe being a murderer situation more complicated was also the about the dumbest idea in the world. Like when Grandma once insisted on the family going out to an expensive restaurant, only for everyone to get food poisoning and race to the bathroom. Because life so needed to be mind-blogging as opposed to being less complicated.

***

Someone tapped my back the next morning at school

after I finished gulping some water by the water fountain. I whirled my body around. Logan was right next to me. But it wasn't his close proximity that caught my attention. Because I was more concerned with the two roses in his hand.

"What are the flowers for?" I asked.

"You." Logan handed me the roses.

"What's the occasion? Don't get me wrong; I like roses. But you know I worry."

I had to be the guy who qualified most of the things I said. Thinking about something being wrong was also natural in light of Grandma's murder, Violet's staged suicide, and Poppy maybe being responsible for both events.

"My mom wants to have you over for dinner," Logan said, averting his gaze.

"What's so bad about that? Are you still concerned about the friction over her not wanting us to date?"

"Nope. I'm more concerned about the timing."

"What are you getting at?"

Yeah. I had no issue with directing the conversation. Logan needed to get to the point since the warning bell would screech in a couple of minutes. I mean, I had no problem with missing Algebra 2, yet Mom wouldn't feel the same way. And I kind of liked being alive and had no desire to be sent to an early grave.

"She wants to have you over tonight," Logan aid.

"That's fine. My family isn't doing anything special tonight. Mom, Dad, Aunt Rita, and Uncle Brad are going to a concert with Tony and Theresa. I passed since classical music isn't exactly my thing."

"I didn't want you to think I was being rude."

"I'd never think that."

He ruffled my hair. "Good. Because I would hate for you to think that."

Sadie pressed her hands together after walking towards us. "Flowers are a nice touch, Logan."

I shook my head, but didn't respond.

Engaging in an argument wouldn't get me anywhere.

My mind was occupied enough with wondering if Poppy was a wicked person.

"I was being genuine," Sadie said. "I have no reason to be a bitch. I've been in a great mood all week."

"Really?" Logan asked.

"One of my paintings was accepted by a gallery in town," Sadie revealed.

I grinned. "That's amazing."

She giggled. "Who knows. Maybe I'll make a successful living as a painter."

This conversation was reason enough to have a warm feeling wash over me. Life was about the simple moments as opposed to having to always anticipate when my family would make the news next. At least in light of Grandma's murder.

***

Logan's mom, or Julia, as she told me to call her, served dinner at exactly six o'clock. The dining room was half the size of my family's dining room, and there were no candles at the center of the table with flickering flames. Although there was a swamp green colored table cloth and the fried chicken and mac and cheese resting in the two dishes on the center of the table weren't burned. And I couldn't forget about Grandma. She would have been the first person to ask where the booze was. Because there were two bottles of seltzer instead of wine next to the food.

I also couldn't forget about the seating arrangements. I sat at the left end of the table while Logan was in the middle and Julia was on the right.

I grabbed one of the seltzer bottles and filled my glass to the top. "The food looks so nice."

"Then dig in," Julia said.

Okay. My bullshit meter broke. I would have suspected Julia threw shade at me with her comment. But I had to be the bigger person by not getting worked up. My relationship with Logan couldn't be thrown away for a quick insult.

I grabbed a piece of fried chicken and scooped some mac and cheese onto my plate before passing both dishes towards Logan.

She grunted. "I understand there was wine at your family's dinner the other day?"

I stole a glance with Logan. Damn. So much for keeping a secret. Then again, I never said he couldn't tell his mom my family served him wine. I just thought it was common sense for him to withhold certain things. Especially in light of how Julia hadn't wanted Logan to date me because of thinking Grandma's death caused too much drama.

"I'm joking. I know Logan is a good kid, and I trust him." Julia took a bite of fried chicken, devouring the skin first.

Please. As if her comment was only intended to be a joke. She left Logan and I hanging for a good thirty seconds. No. it was more like a minute.

"You shouldn't have let him come over to my house if you had reservations about my character." I took a bite of the mac and cheese. Wow. The mixture of three cheese sauce pleased my picky taste buds. The hint of mayonnaise was also nice because that provided a balance to the cheese.

Logan gripped the right side of his head. Although there wasn't much hair to hold onto to calm his nerves. He had a shorter haircut than me.

"Yes, I did in the beginning. But my son has a mind of his own," Julia said.

"There's something you should know," I said.

"Casey, please!" Logan said.

It didn't matter how mature I acted. I was human, and that meant not being perfect. I also needed to stand up for myself. It wasn't like I wanted to accuse Julia of being a terrible person. I just needed to be firm since Julia needed to be know I wasn't someone to mess with. Like that time Grandma stood up to her mechanic after Dad implied she was getting ripped off. And the anger was worth it. Grandma's subsequent visit after telling off her mechanic was on the house.

Her eyebrows knitted together. "I'm listening."

"I love Logan and won't take shit from anyone. We make each other happy, and I intend on treating him right," I said.

"That's good enough for me." Julia raised her glass before guzzling half of it.

***

I returned home from the dinner sometime later, only to be greeted by the lights being off. And I winced. I so loved spending time in the dark. Enough theatrics for now, though. Perhaps Uncle Brad, Aunt Rita, Mom, Dad, Tony, and Theresa were still at the concert while Poppy was up to whatever she did in the evenings.

My heart thumped after I flicked on the lights by the front door before someone gripped my neck. No. No. No. There couldn't be an intruder in my family's mansion. Life was supposed to get less dramatic because my family didn't need to make the news again.

Wait. I might not have known everything, but I couldn't die. So, I summoned all the energy I had, and stomped on the person's right foot, before running towards the stairwell.

I titled my head. The person sported a ski mask, black hoodie, sweatpants, and shoes. And as much as I would have liked to know the sex of my attacker, I didn't. The ski mask covered the person's face, and black hoodie and sweatpants were bagging, making it difficult to know the person's exact physical stature.

The stranger rushed over to me as soon as I almost stepped onto the bottom step.

Fuck. I shouldn't have allowed myself to get distracted with what my attacker looked like, and made a real exit.

One swift forward motion made my back slam against the wall. The person soon gripped my neck. The hold tightened, making me want scream. Yet I couldn't the words or energy to articulate how I felt. Not when the person was trying to crush my windpipe with every amount of pressure possible. Yes. The amount of force pressing against my neck was worse than a python constricting its poor defenseless prey.

Shit. I was gonna die, and there was nothing I could do about this asshole choking the life out of me since the grip around my neck was tighter than when the person first tried to strangle me.

Fuck it. I might not have had magic, but I wasn't gonna give up. I needed to put up a fight.

Slamming the person in the head with my head took all the energy I had. But my response was perfect. The intruder fell backwards a few feet before slipping and thudding against the oak floor.

The front door opened. But I didn't stand. Defending myself was one thing. But I needed to catch my breath. Although I did look up at the person.

"What are you doing here, Logan?" I asked.

His lips quivered. "You forgot your iPhone."

"You don't know how glad I am to see you," I took the iPhone from him before placing it in my pocket.

"What the hell happened? I've never seen you out of breath before?" Logan demanded.

"Someone tried to kill me."

He shifted his gaze before looking back at me. "The person is gone, Casey."

Moving my gaze to where the masked intruder had been revealed the person was no longer there. Damn. Looking like I suffered from hallucinations would make this evening even more wonderful. I so wanted to be declared crazy and locked up in a mental institution.

I sobbed. "You have to believe me."

"Relax. I believe you."

Logan sat on the floor next to me. I collapsed into his chest and sobbed more while he ran his fingers through my hair and the other rubbed my back.

I would find the culprit once my pulse returned to normal, though. I just had to. It was a promise.

CHAPTER 32

"You really are a genius," I said.

Logan and I continued walking through the park on Main Street in town. But he didn't say anything. At least for the moment. Although I didn't blame him for his silence. And my reasoning wasn't even because of the slight chill in the air and the red, orange, yellow, and brown leaves scattered in various parts on the ground. Pondering how the calendar officially switched to fall could wait till later. It hadn't even been a full twenty-four hours since my attack, and I could only speculate if Logan had the same amount of fear trembling through his body that I did.

I had no issue with sounding extreme. I was allowed to make a big deal out of almost dying. It wasn't like I went around demanding sympathy from people. I just needed to feel safe again. Although I shouldn't have glossed over how Logan was the only person who knew about yesterday's event. Hating dishonesty was one thing. But there was nothing wrong with the occasional sin of omission. Like when Grandma failed to disclose her publishing company was being audited by the IRS three years ago. Because the expression on Dad's face after the revelation was priceless.

He tilted his head. "And why is that?"

"I'd never have thought to go on the internet to look up Violet's ex-husband's contact information."

"It's the next logical thing to do. We need to figure out if he lied when he recanted. Although I'm not sure if I should be insulted by your comment."

"What are you talking about?"

He gave me a mock frown. "Did you need to qualify your genius comment?"

"I didn't mean anything bad by it. I just meant I was in no condition to be the next Albert Einstein," I said.

He smirked. "Everyone needs help every now and then."

Yup. I couldn't disagree with Logan regardless of how some people might have been too embarrassed to ask for help. Suffering in silence wasn't about one of the dumbest things a person could do. If a problem had an easy solution, then considering it had to be done. Like if someone was drowning and was offering help. Refusing assistance wouldn't have accomplished anything.

So, yeah. Just because I was too scared to go to the police about my attack—I consumed enough pop culture to know I needed to proceed carefully, because I could look like the crazy one if people discovered I was investigating Grandma's murder—didn't mean my boyfriend couldn't help me. He could.

"Do you want a hot chocolate and apple cider donut?" Logan asked. "It'd be my treat."

Damn. I was an open book, and there was no hope of getting anything past Logan. Because I was unsure if I felt comfortable with Logan paying for something. Then again, there was something to be said for small acts of kindness. A nicety could sometimes be a nicety. Logan probably still noticed the fear radiating form my eyes, and wanted to distract me from yesterday's attack.

I smiled. "Sure. That'd be great."

"We'll have two hot chocolates and two apple cider

donuts." Logan grabbed his wallet from his jacket pocket, and took out a ten-dollar bill. He then handed it to the man.

The vendor gave the two hot chocolates and apple cider donuts to Logan before give a customary good-bye smile that cashiers and other people in the service industry always seemed to do.

"Thanks," I said, taking the hot chocolate and apple cider donut from Logan.

"My pleasure."

I bit into the donut while Logan and I scurried. The mixture of tart apple flavor, doughy texture, and sweetness from the powdered sugar illuminated every cell in my mouth. A bit of powdered sugar even stuck to my lips. But I didn't flinch. I was a human being; not God. And that meant I was allowed to be imperfect. Although Grandma would have lectured me if she were here. Getting food on my face wouldn't have fit her prim and proper image.

"You have something on your lip," Logan said.

"I know."

He stopped. "I'll get it."

He wet his right index finger with his tongue before stroking my lip. And it was only a matter of seconds before my heart thumped faster while I looked into his eyes. Yup. Our current eye contact resembled a perfect Hallmark moment. However, we needed to get with the program ASAP. Thinking Violet's husband would have waited for us all afternoon was naïve. He must have had a life that didn't always include agreeing to a meeting with teens on a whim.

"Thanks for meeting us," I said a couple of minutes later after we approached a park bench.

He tugged at the sides of his trench coat. "No problem."

Logan sighed. "We understand this might be a delicate subject, but we need closure since we were friends with Violet."

Okay. Fine. Logan embellished when he contacted Chip. But he didn't mean any harm. The subtle approach was smart. Being too direct would have scared Chip off, which would have left Logan and I with nothing. Like that time Grandma told me about going out to a bar and how she was pretty sure she scared off a guy by being too desperate.

"What can I do for you two?" Chip asked.

"Why did you recant your statement to the police after Violet's 'suicide'?" I asked. "Because you initially backed up her alibi when they arrested her."

I just had to ask a loaded question. Logan not frightening Chip away was one thing, but we hadn't agreed to meet Chip to discuss the weather.

"I wouldn't have met you two if I knew you wanted to talk about this," Chip asked.

I glared at Chip. "I don't think Violet killed her mother or committed suicide."

Chip grunted. "Neither do I. She really met with me the night she was murdered because she needed a loan."

"Then why recant?" Logan snapped.

"Because someone called threatening to tell my new wife, Violet and I were having an affair, which is believable considering I cheated on Violet when we were married" Chip revealed.

Interesting. Violet told me the truth about her ex-husband cheating on her, thus further proving she hadn't killed Grandma.

I furrowed an eyebrow. "Who?"

"I don't know. The phone number was blocked and the voice was that distorted generic thing people use when trying to disguise themselves." Chip cracked his knuckles.

"Can you think of anything else?" I asked.

His jaw trembled. "No. And I'm sorry, but I have to go. Best of luck to you two."

He wobbled away without another. Whatever. Logan and I got what we wanted because we now had proof that

Violet wasn't the killer. Sure. We couldn't go marching into the police station since Chip's credibility waned as a result of changing his stance. But we knew the truth, and that was enough for now.

***

Sadie and I walked through the school hallway the following morning. We also happened to be en route to Logan's locker, but that was a minor detail. The point was, we were getting quality best friend time.

Some ideas needed to be stated no matter how obvious they sounded. Remembering what life was supposed to be like perplexed me as a result of being so caught up in Grandma's murder and Violet's "suicide."

"Anyway, you have no idea how much this means to me that my painting will debut at the Foxy Lane Gallery in town tonight," Sadie said.

"Being a writer counts as an artistic profession, and I understand the need for validation."

"And it'll be so great, especially since you, Logan, and Tony will be there to support me."

I agreed to go to Sadie's art debut. Whatever. It wasn't like she got me drunk and made me sign my life away in some sketchy arrangement. Nope. I was just supporting a friend.

"What about Theresa?" I asked.

Her gaze widened. "Weren't you paying attention? She has a Spanish Test she has to study for tomorrow."

***

Tony, Logan, Sadie, and I stood by Sadie's painting the following night for moral support as promised at the art show.

Although I started having sympathy pangs for Sadie a few minutes ago. Nobody looked at her painting yet. Eve-

157

ryone was too busy at the wine and snack tables in addition to looking at the other ten various paintings scattered throughout the room on the wall.

Sadie's painting was the most original, though, and my opinion had nothing to do with being her best friend. Her painting was a rainbow self-portrait. Kind of like the painting of Grandma hanging on the upstairs wall back at my family's mansion. Something exciting existed about Sadie using non-local colors because it showed she wasn't afraid to take a risk.

Tony bit his lip. "I'm sure someone will look at your painting soon."

Damn.

Tony had more guts than I realized. I would have been too timid to address nobody wanting to look at her painting if I were Tony. But I wasn't Tony, and didn't have to bear the brunt of Sadie's nerves. Because I so wanted to cause more problems.

"I hope so," Sadie said.

Logan adjusted his bowtie. "All great artists face resistance."

Taking a moment to ponder Logan's comment would have happened in any other situation. But not now. Turning my head made my stomach churn as numerous thoughts raced through my mind. Yet none of the thoughts mattered compared to my actual problem. Poppy stood outside the gallery window. I blinked, and she was gone when I opened my eyes. Although my pulse pounded in my ears. I only needed one guess to realize I wasn't insane.

"Something wrong?" Logan asked.

"I just saw Poppy standing outside the gallery," I whispered into his ear while attempting to ignore the pulsing sensation in my fingers from blood pumping through my body faster.

"What do you want to do?" Logan asked.

"I don't know. But now I'm really alarmed. I think I also spotted Poppy in the park yesterday when we talked to

Chip," I revealed.

Yup. I never had an issue with omitting the occasional fact since my same stance was still correct. I wasn't unreliable as a result of holding back about being responsible for something terrible. I just needed time to process events.

Sadie gave us a dirty look. "What are you two mumbling about?"

"Nothing," I said.

I might have been a lot of things, but I wasn't a jerk. And that meant not ruining Sadie's night. Worrying about being stalked could wait till later like every other problem I procrastinated.

CHAPTER 33

Sadie and I sat at one of the tables in front of the high school's main entrance the next morning. The stacked together clouds in the sky told the real story, though. And it wasn't because there wasn't a drop of sunlight radiating from the sky that made me skeptical. The saturated grey colored clouds were what made my shoulders shudder. Like the time Grandma was in NYC and had to walk sixteen blocks in pouring rain because no taxi would stop for her.

Shit. Sadie had once again been talking for the last few minutes. Yet I had no idea what she was saying.

"You really are something else," Sadie said.

I glanced at her. "What do you mean?"

"I can tell when you aren't paying attention."

"I have no idea what you're talking about."

"Don't bullshit me."

I sucked in a breath. "I have a lot on my mind."

She giggled. "I would ask you if you want to talk about it. But I'm still basking in my reversal of fortunes."

"Come again?" I asked.

"My painting sold, and I made a thousand dollars."

My eyes widened. "I'm so proud of you."

"Thanks. Anyway, are you sure you don't want to talk about whatever is on your mind?"

I swallowed the lump in my throat. "I'm good."

Sure. I couldn't fault Sadie for being concerned about me. But I didn't want to ramble about how I still didn't know who killed Grandma and staged Violet's death as a suicide.

Yes. I understood the importance of not being bratty and having humility for the discoveries Logan and I made. However, we only had a bunch of pieces, as opposed to knowing the whole story. We still had no proof that Poppy killed Grandma. Stalking me was the only thing Poppy was guilty of—fort the moment, at least.

Shit. There were times I couldn't shake wanting to pinch myself. Life had spun out of control. Like last Thanksgiving when Grandma had one too many Gin and Tonics, and thought the room was spinning. And Dad might as well have screamed at Grandma for her behavior. The contempt glowing from his eyes made my heart thump faster.

"I had my moment, and we can talk about you if you want." Sadie grabbed a hair tie from her purse before running her fingers through her hair. She then put it up in a ponytail.

Wow. I wasn't the only stressed person. Sifting her fingers through her hair, accentuated its greasy texture. Almost as if she forgot to use conditioner. Because Grandma would have given her a dirty look if she was here. Apparently, hair very important to women. According to Grandma that was. She was the same woman who once believed November had 31 days.

"That's fine," I said.

"I won't be mad if you want to talk about your grandma."

"You worry too much."

"Have you met me?"

I forced laughter. "Good point."

Rain splattered onto the ground before the wind swooshed faster. And it was only a matter of seconds before purple tinged lightning zig-zagged across the sky. A clap of thunder roared, making me almost cover my ears.

Great. I so needed to get rained on. Because I wanted to jump for joy at the opportunity of being drenched in water.

"Congrats; you were right. Maybe you should be a weatherman." Sadie shoved everything into her backpack before zipping it up and standing.

"He'd make a cute weatherman," Logan said after walking up to us.

Sadie and I didn't gesture at him to sit down. Nope. We started trekking towards the high school's main entrance after the rain pattered onto the ground louder and faster. Logan lagged behind since he spent several seconds tying his sneaker.

***

"It'd be nice if the weather cleared up," Logan said.

Fog clung to the air hours later while Logan continued driving us to the inn Violet stayed at until her death. I would have even compared the fog to a thick blob of spider webs a spider would have oozed in a horror movie since the visibility was that bad.

But I needed to focus on our latest step in being amateur detectives. There was no harm in talking to the inn manager in hopes of finding out if he ever saw Poppy at the inn.

Accusing Poppy of planting the gun in Violet's room wasn't practical without proof. But it was important to have a good working theory. I mean, I had no problem with apologizing if Poppy turned out to be innocent. And I could have kicked myself. I stronger person would have been more vigorous with uncovering the truth about Grandma's death. But not me. And my reasoning wasn't because being seventeen meant I was naïve. A part of me died the day Grandma was murdered, and I didn't know if I'd ever get that part of myself back

He took his eyes off the road for a beat. "Something wrong? You seem pretty quiet."

"I'll tell you another time."

"Fair enough."

"Although I'm glad I came up with the plan," I said.

He snorted. "I never doubted that you're resourceful."

"Thanks."

Logan stopped at a red light. His cursing was even justified. The light changed from yellow to red right as we approached it. Although the car in front of us took too long to move.

And it wasn't odd we had now been in the car for a good fifteen minutes. We left for the inn from school; not home. School was on the other end of town, as opposed to my family's mansion, which couldn't have been any closer to the inn if it tried. It wasn't like the time Grandma and I went to Savannah, Georgia for my 13th birthday and we were three days late checking into the hotel.

"At least Sadie sold her painting. I could have sworn she looked like she was about to murder someone last night," Logan said.

"Don't be so dramatic."

"You weren't afraid of her?"

I picked at one of my nails. "No."

The light changed to green, but Logan didn't notice. At least not at first. Although I wasn't one to talk either. I hadn't discovered the light changed until the car behind us honked several times. Yet I would just take in a deep breath. The important thing was Logan didn't curse again like when we missed the light. Although I would take a second to mention Grandma. She hated cursing like Aunt Rita and always told people she didn't care what they said or did as long as they didn't swear. And I couldn't fault Grandma for seeming old fashioned by having contempt for profanity. That trait defined part of her personality because Grandma would have been a different person if she didn't have a problem with swearing. But the dirty looks she gave when people used "nasty" words was excessive. Using "proper" language was one thing. But she wasn't the speech police.

Logan pulled into the parking lot a minute later, and there was a good chance I would get left behind in the car if I didn't silence my thoughts. And that would have been bad. Logan and I were in this together, and that meant not making a move about Grandma's murder/Violet's staged suicide/Poppy possibly being the killer situation without consulting Logan first.

"What can I do for you?" the receptionist asked after Logan and I shuffled into the lobby.

I grabbed my iPhone from my jacket pocket. I pulled up my photo app and scrolled through all the photos before finding a picture of Poppy.

"I was just wondering if you have ever seen this woman here?" I asked, showing the receptionist Poppy's photo.

The man remained silent for the longest. Logan and I exchanged a glance. Although we couldn't complain. The person was doing us a favor.

"Once," said the man.

Logan raised his brow. "When?"

"The night of your grandmother's 60th birthday," the man said, looking at me. "I'll never be able to forget about that day. Anyone who was anyone in this town wanted an invite to the party."

A lump lingered in my throat.

Shit. I didn't need to be more suspicious of Poppy than I was. Yet I shouldn't have complained. I wanted answers, and had to be prepared with the possibility of not liking what he heard. Like that time Grandma asked her lawyer about the exact amount of money she owed the IRS after the audit revealed she needed to pay more taxes. Apparently, three million dollars was highway robbery in Grandma's mind.

"Can you tell us anything else?" Logan asked.

"I didn't tell the police this because I didn't want get in trouble or lose my job. But the lady gave me a bribe to go into room 313," said the man.

Ding. Ding. Ding. Room 313 was Violet's room, and I now had another link to her and Poppy--whether I wanted it or not.

Logan tugged at the sides of his jacket. "Did she say what she wanted?"

"She needed to return something to a friend that didn't want the person to know she took. Anyway, you have to promise not to tell anyone," said the man. "Being honest with you two is one thing, but I've never been a fan of cops. Not after they planted drugs on my brother. So, no reason to make my life more complicated than necessary."

I nodded. "Sure. I'm very discreet."

"Wonderful," said someone.

That voice! Poppy stood by the elevator a few feet away from us.

"What are you two doing here?" Poppy asked after walking towards us.

The receptionist looked at Logan and I before Poppy glanced at the man.

"We wanted to know how much a room costs," Logan said.

Poppy folded her arms. "Why do you need a room?"

"Do we really have to spell it out?" Logan asked.

Poppy winked. "Oh! You wanna have sex."

"Not so loud." I clenched my jaw. Yeah. My business didn't need to be broadcasted across the entire lobby. Sex was private and Poppy didn't need to muddy my relationship with Logan by creating awkwardness.

She clapped her mouth. "My apologies."

"It's fine," Logan said without hesitation.

Frown lines formed on Poppy's face while she looked the receptionist in the eye. He then averted his gaze by looking at his computer screen. Although he hadn't fooled Poppy, Logan, or I. Being unable to make eye contact told me everything I needed to know.

But Poppy didn't wait around to make more banter since her high heels stabbed the ground while she approached the lobby. The placard—consisting of the inn's name—jingled against the door after Poppy stepped outside. Yet I couldn't shake the scornful look she gave the receptionist moments earlier.

Fleshing out my thought meant admitting the window for proving Poppy's innocence was closing faster and faster.

Fuck. I still couldn't admit I might have been living with a murderer until we had both more proof and certainty. I just couldn't accept the possible reality.

I sighed even louder than when I had earlier in Logan's car. Expressing doubt about falling down the rabbit hole that was Poppy's guilt was ill timed. It was a little too late to call off playing detective. I couldn't un-learn my concerns. Although I could pretend to hope I would get a good night sleep to settle all the "noises" in my head.

CHAPTER 34

Grandma once told me if it feels like you're being watched, then there's a good chance someone is watching you. Like that time Grandma went to Paris seven years ago and a man followed her for fourteen blocks. Apparently, she was convinced the guy wanted to kill her. And now my heart once again pounded inside my chest as I was in the middle of doing my homework at my bedroom desk several hours after running into Poppy at the inn.

My bedroom door creaked. Great. Poppy entered my bedroom. Yet I shouldn't have made an internal judgment. I still needed concrete proof about her. However, I was pretty sure Grandma would have made some quirky comment about going with my intuition if she were here.

My eyes lit up. "What do you want, Poppy?"

"Can't I chat with my favorite cousin?" Poppy strutted into my bedroom, closing the remaining distance between us. She was now less than a foot away from me. And she was close even enough to me that my eyes burned from whatever perfume she used.

Hang on. She answered a question with another question, which meant my bullshit meter should have gone off. I wasn't clueless—I understood why someone would answer a question with another question.

I closed my textbook and notebook before shoving them to the side. "What's up?"

She sucked in a breath. "I didn't mean to embarrass you earlier today."

"Doesn't matter."

"You seemed flabbergasted."

"I take after Grandma. You know she always used to be dramatic."

Her eyes bulged. "Her death was a tragedy."

"It was."

"Are you and Logan still playing amateur detectives?" Poppy asked.

Interesting. She remembered the conversation from that day on the beach. And I shouldn't have had a lowered jaw. She was only in her twenties, and was way too young to suffer from memory problems. I also would have even gone as a tangent about Grandma worrying about losing her memory in the past.

"Well?" she demanded.

"Yes, we are." I stood after pushing in my chair.

"Why? Don't you think you should just leave the past in the past?"

I folded my arms. "What's it to you?"

"I care about you."

Please. As if. Poppy shouldn't have insulted my intelligence by feigning concern. I might have been a lot of things, but being a writer entailed knowing how to read people. And that meant I wasn't the only one in the room with increased breathing.

"I'm serious," Poppy continued.

"Why are you so bothered? It's not like I'm bitching to you all the time about how I don't think Violet killed

Grandma."

She shook her head. "Doesn't matter. You shouldn't concern yourself with such foolishness."

"I can look after myself, thanks."

She put her hands on her hips. "What would your mother say if she discovered what you and Logan have been up to?"

I snorted. "It's going to take more than a threat to scare me."

"It wasn't a threat. It was a fact."

"What do you want?" I asked.

"I want to understand what's going through your mind."

I put my hands in my pockets "There are a lot of facts that don't add up."

"Such as?"

I forced in a deep breath. Sure. Poppy and I had already been talking for a few minutes. But I needed to decide whether to just let the mater go or continue down this new rabbit hole. Because I shouldn't have thought twice about my response given that I was Casey the Curious.

"Violet's ex-husband said someone pressured him into recanting, which means she really did have an alibi," I revealed.

She nibbled on the inside of her lip. "I'd be careful if I were you."

"Meaning?"

"Going down rabbit holes can be dangerous, and I'd hate for anything bad to happen to you."

Hmmm. Maybe we had more in common than I realized if she also loved *Alice and Wonderland* and used the rabbit hole phrase too.

***

"Poppy is getting more unhinged," I blurted the following morning.

"Explain." Logan slammed his locker door shut. But I wouldn't begrudge him for being dramatic. Nope. We had more important things to talk about.

"She threatened me last night."

"Poppy did what?"

"She's hiding something, and it's more than flunking out of school."

Logan grimaced. "She did give me the creeps yesterday."

"I'm sorry I dragged you into this…"

Yeah. I would still apologize for anything and everything. Even when I hadn't done anything awful. I wasn't oblivious to how Logan's life was more complex as a result of making him help me find out who killed Grandma and Violet. Wait. I didn't make him do anything. Logan offered to help, and I just happened to take him up on it.

He pushed my chin up. "Don't ever apologize for anything."

I laughed. Disbelief still jolted my body. Being an amateur detective shouldn't have been my life. Yet it was, and there was nothing I could do about it until I found definitive proof about Poppy.

He raised his eyebrows. "What do you want to do next?"

"It's Wednesday."

"So?"

"Poppy is never home on Wednesday night, and we should figure out what she's up to."

The outside hammering rain continued echoing through the school hallway while Logan stared at me. A student also happened to scurry by despite how being in a hurry was a mistake. The guy slipped on the floor. But he just banged his ass against the ground as opposed to something more serious. I would have offered to help him up or gone on another digression. But not when Logan hadn't responded to my comment.

"What if you don't like the answer you get?" he mumbled.

I sighed. "It'll be better than ambiguity. I can't keep playing guessing games with whether Poppy is harmless or a monster."

***

The orange and pink had pretty much vanished from the sky hours later after Logan and I followed Poppy to a restaurant on some sketchy side street in town.

Okay. Fine. Sketchy was a harsh word. But I was just emulating Grandma. She always used to refer to this side of town as sketchy as a result of the cheaper restaurants. Yet there wasn't a crime problem in this neighbor.

"I wonder who she's meeting." Logan took off his jacket and put it on the driver seat floor.

Yeah. We took his car for Operation Stalk Poppy. I didn't want to tempt fate by bringing my Mercedes. And it wasn't thinking Grandma was right about looking down on this part of town. I just didn't want Poppy to notice me. Because it didn't matter if I lived in an affluent suburb. Any sign of wealth still attracted attention.

Poppy glanced at her watch. She hadn't moved from her spot in front of the restaurant. But now was no time to chastise her for the growing frown line on Poppy's face. I just had to hope today's mission would lead to an important discovery.

Logan squeezed my hand. "It's okay if we don't find anything. I still believe you about Poppy."

"What the fuck?" I wasn't responding to him. Something just caught my eye. My jaw remained lowered. There was no way I saw what I did. Sure. I didn't live under a rock and sometimes watched television shows and movies with copious amounts of sex, swearing, and violence. But my eyes must have played tricks on me since I wasn't ready to deal with the truth.

"I can't believe it," Logan said.

Good to know I wasn't the only with shock radiating from my body. There was no way Poppy kissed the man just she did. Someone had to have slipped me a drug when I wasn't looking.

He shifted his weight. "Do you wanna discuss it?"

"There's not much to say."

"You can squeal if you want."

I didn't speak. And it wasn't that I wanted to drag out this moment. I didn't. I would have had no problem with being proven wrong if I knew in advance about tonight's shocking reveal.

"Fine," Logan said, pausing for a beat. "I'll say it if you won't. Poppy is one fucked up person if she's having an affair with her stepfather."

Yup. Logan hadn't misspoken even though wishing he had tempted me. Poppy just met Uncle Brad in front of the restaurant and had a quick kiss after they looked and realized nobody was watching. Although I should have been glad they hadn't realized Logan and I saw their kiss. Life was complicated, and a good night sleep couldn't come fast enough.

CHAPTER 35

I entered the kitchen the next afternoon and grabbed a water bottle from the fridge, only to discover Mom with a disapproving look.

"Did someone die?" I asked.

Shit. I hadn't learned my lesson about making a crude statement in light of Grandma's death. But I needed relief after discovering Poppy's embrace with Uncle Brad last night. Almost like that time when Grandma once told me she spent an hour composing an email only to delete by mistake and I wanted nothing more than to chuckle. I excused myself, and burst into a hysterical fit of laughter.

"Poppy talked to me," Mom said.

Having someone cause problems for me was just what I needed. Hold on. Waiting to find out what she told Mom was best. Jumping to conclusions would make my life more complex, and that would only cause more drama.

Mom scratched the side of her head. "She said you've been very upset about Grandma's death and are obsessing about how you don't think Violet killed her."

Wow. Poppy had more balls than I realized. She had quite the nerve to meddle by talking to Mom. Doing so only proved she had something to hide, yet I dismissed the rage shooting through my body. Acting based on an emotional reaction would only make life messier. And that would have been a big mistake. Life wasn't a yard sale where I could buy more emotional problems.

"You shouldn't trust her, Mom," I said without cringing.

Her gaze narrowed. "Why?"

"Poppy isn't the person she claims to be. She flunked out of school and has been keeping it a secret since last winter."

Poppy could fuck with me, and I could fuck with her.

I refused to let anyone put me in a corner. Yes. I still wasn't clear what Poppy's motive was for killing Grandma. Flunking out of school was only a guess in addition to how the new revelation about her affair with Uncle Brad added another possible motive to the mix.

***

Bugs kept buzzing around my face a couple hours later while I swatted them en route to Logan's house. He texted me about wanting me to come over and meet him in the backyard. Black also draped the night sky, which meant an elevated pulse. But I was pretty sure nothing bad would happen.

Sure. It was evening. However, harming someone seemed easier behind closed doors.

I needed to get a grip ASAP. Letting my mind wander more meant ignoring the neon green tent in Logan's front yard. The zipper squeaked, tracing the perimeter of the tent's opening. Logan then stepped out of the tent.

I chuckled. "What's with the cryptic text?"

"I thought we could use a date night."

Thank goodness for Logan. I didn't want to say anything because being bratty was foolish, but Logan and I hadn't had much time for romance. Yes. Something hot existed about "playing" amateur detective with him. But it still would have been nice to go to the movies, coffee, or dinner. Yet I hadn't made a big deal out of needing more couple time. I was secure enough in my relationship with Logan to understand everything would be fine.

I stepped into the tent. There were several blankets on top of each other in addition to a pillow behind them. There was also a gigantic bowl of popcorn and a bottle of diet ginger ale with two cups. Although those items weren't the reason for me cracking a smile. A laptop with a *Run, Lola, Run* DVD container rested a few feet away from the refreshments. Wow. Maybe I influenced Logan more than I realized. There was nothing more romantic than him owing a copy of *Run, Lola, Run*.

His cheeks flushed. "Don't laugh, but I bought my own copy."

I winked. "I'm impressed."

"I thought we could use a break from all the mystery."

"Thank you," I said before sitting down in front of the pillows.

Logan followed my lead and sat too. "I'm your boyfriend; you don't have to thank me for anything."

"I don't mean to kill the mood, but there's something you should know."

"I'm listening."

"Poppy tried to drive a wedge between my mom and I." I took a handful of popcorn. My taste buds were electrified as I munched on the popcorn as a result of the buttery goodness. Appreciating the flavor wasn't just some arbitrary detail. Grandma always complained about popcorn sometimes being too dry, and I agreed with her. There was nothing more annoying than a parched throat.

Logan exhaled a breath. "Sorry to hear that."

"Forget about it. Poppy is tomorrow's problem."

"A part of me was also selfish because I didn't just want a date night. I wanted to chat too," Logan said after he took the DVD out and inserted it into the laptop.

My jaw twitched. "Did I do something wrong?"

"I didn't realize it right away," Logan said. "But you seemed uncomfortable at the inn lobby, and it wasn't just because of cousin dearest."

Trusting my intuition meant realizing there was a good chance Logan and I were about to have a sex talk. Yet we couldn't even if we were in a respectful relationship. Discussing sex was awkward. Besides, I blushed too much in the inn lobby.

"What's your point?" I asked, being careful not to raise my voice.

He shrugged. "I thought we should talk about it."

"Okay…"

"I don't wanna assume anything. But you are a teenage boy like me."

So much for not stating the obvious. His comment was a guarantee for more embarrassment. Because thoughts about sex had crossed my mind. I just hadn't taken the time to process them. Grandma's and Violet's deaths seemed like the more urgent issue.

"Yes," I stammered. "I wonder what it'd be like if we slept together."

He huffed. "I'm sorry. This is just as difficult for you, as it is for me. I'm not saying we have to sleep together tonight. I just want to touch base on the issue."

I chuckled. "Yes. I would like to sleep with you at some point. But I don't think tonight is the night."

He let out nervous laughter too. "Agreed."

"There's one more thing I should say."

"And what's that?"

I squeezed his hand. "You never have to be afraid about discussing anything with me."

His gaze narrowed. "Really?"

"Yes. I promise I won't bite your head off."

"Great."

"Although I need to make another thing clear. Not sleeping with you tonight doesn't mean I don't wanna do other things." I leaned closer, making my heart flutter. The amount of time I spent with Logan wouldn't stop blood from traveling through my body faster when it came to him.

Allowing myself to be close to someone made my stomach twist in ten different directions. Even a simple kiss on the lips like right now meant allowing myself to be vulnerable. And the risk was worth it. There was nothing like him stroking my hair and looking deep into my eyes after kissing. Or maybe I listened to Grandma too much when she went on about all the romance novels she read. Nope. Grandma was right. Romance was like Christmas. It made the world a brighter place because of creating hope. Even when a noise rustled through the air while I continued making out with my boyfriend. And the sound wasn't the wind whistling or an animal noise. Nope. This noise was subtler. Like the crunching of feet against the leaf infested ground. The faint silhouette of someone's shadow reflecting from outside the tent didn't help either.

CHAPTER 36

Chatting with Theresa needed to happen the following morning. It wasn't even that I had anything important to say. I just wanted quality time with my other best friend.

I hadn't forgotten about the all the times she went with me to Starbucks over the summer when Sadie was out of town. Although I wouldn't lie about one thing. I needed to get a grip. Because I knew what I saw last night. Someone lurked outside the tent while we made out, and I didn't need three guesses to think about who it was. The old me might have continued giving Poppy the benefit of the doubt. But too many things happened that couldn't be ignored. Like Violet's ex-husband being threatened to recant his statement by an anonymous person, Poppy's earring in Grandma's bedroom, Uncle Brad giving her a false alibi, her flunking out of college, her being involved with Uncle Brad, and bribing the inn receptionist.

Figuring out what all the clues meant would have been nice, though. Yes. I had a good idea of who Poppy really was. Yet I still needed a motive. Or maybe it didn't matter what her reasoning was. She seemed guilty, and that should have been enough. However, I needed to figure out what to do with my suspicions. Convincing adults of Poppy's guilt would be as difficult of a battle as my amateur sleuthing with Logan. Adults didn't always believe what teenagers told them, and I could only imagine about getting a few frowns or furrowed eyebrows. Violet was the easy explanation, and everyone seemed to have moved on from Grandma's murder. I, of all people, would know. Almost nobody stared and whispered at me when I was in town now. Because I so wanted my family to always dominate town gossip.

Theresa giggled. "Are you just gonna stand there?"

Crap. I forgot I wanted to talk to Theresa.

"Nobody will think anything about my tangents when I'm a famous writer," I said.

"Keep dreaming."

I rolled my eyes.

"I was teasing," Theresa said, smirking.

"You seem extra happy this morning."

"I took your advice." Her mouth widened more, revealing her well-aligned teeth. Wow. So much for how she used to complain about braces.

"About what?" I asked.

She closed her locker. "About fashion. I'm entering the competition with the local designer Carrie Marshall. The winner gets to design a new line in Carrie's company."

"I never told you to enter the contest," I said while Theresa and I began walking down the school hallway.

She snorted. "I know. But you told me to pursue fashion more."

"I'm glad I could help."

"That's not all."

I nodded.

"I would have never found out about the contest if I

hadn't joined the high school's fashion club," Theresa continued.

I nudged her shoulder. "Look at you. I'm so proud of you for branching out and reaching your potential."

"I'm still not done."

I tugged my backpack straps. "There's more?"

"I met a guy in the club, and I'm 100 percent sure he's straight."

We turned the corner in the hallway.

"I thought you didn't need a relationship?" I asked.

She flipped her hair. "It turns out you can have it all."

"I'm happy for you."

***

"I wanted to apologize," Julia said.

I just returned from a walk around the neighborhood hours later in the afternoon when Logan's mother gestured at me to come over to her driveway.

"For what?" I asked.

She pursed her lips. "For any awkwardness that there might have been between us."

Interesting. Perhaps Julia and I were more alike than I realized. Pointless apologies were something I was all too familiar with.

"Don't worry about it. Standing up to you at the dinner was enough," I said.

Yes. Logan's mom no longer bothered me. Not when Poppy might have killed Grandma. Not when I still wanted to find Poppy's motive. Not when I wondered if Poppy would go to jail. And not when my beads of sweat would still stick to my body when thinking about Logan's sex talk. Because his talk caused the issue of contemplating of knowing when the right moment to have sex would be.

She rubbed her hair, which was wrapped in a bun. "I know. I just wanted to clear the air."

"It's all good."

"That's not all."

Damn. I just didn't understand. People could never get to the point by mentioning their true intentions. Not when dancing around the issue was easier.

"You need to be very careful about who you spend time with," Julia continued.

"You're gonna have be more direct."

"My problem was never with you." She looked down at the ground. A spider was now only a few inches away from her. But she didn't scream or recoil. She just crushed the spider with one stomp of her foot. Wow. A part of me respected her more. Most people would have run in the opposite direction of spiders. I of all people understood that point. I still couldn't watch the second *Harry Potter* because of the enormous spiders. "It was with your cousin Poppy."

My eyebrows inched up.

"Poppy doesn't seem like she has it together. At least the night of your grandma's birthday when she grunted and talked to herself while walking towards her car." She paused for a beat and unscrewed the cap of her water bottle. Although it might as well have taken her one million years to take the top off. I had never seen someone other than Grandma take so long to do a simple thing. She then took a good chug of water before putting the cap back on. And Julia didn't just put the cap back on. She twisted it all the way around so it wouldn't be loose. "But I was more afraid for my mailbox than anything else. She pulled out of your driveway so fast that I thought she would take it out."

"Why are you telling me this?" I asked.

"I thought you should be careful. I mean, it's probably nothing. I imagine your grandma's death has been stressful for your entire family. But it's better to be safe than sorry."

"You probably shouldn't tell Poppy about this conversation."

Thinking Logan's mom would inform Poppy about

this conversation might have made me seem like a tool. But I couldn't help covering myself in light of Poppy "gossiping" to Mom about me being obsessed with Grandma's death.

She snickered. "Don't be ridiculous. I'm not an idiot."

A beeping sound echoed several times. Although my iPhone wasn't vibrating. Julia's phone was the culprit, and I wasn't trying to blame her because of any lingering resentment. She had actually taken her iPhone out of her pocket and answered the call. In fact, she already finished answering the call. The iPhone was no longer in her hand. Nope. She just had a concerned expression on her face.

"Everything okay?" I asked.

"That was the police. Logan's been in a car accident."

***

"I just hope the plan works," I said the following afternoon.

Logan and I stood against the wall after the turner in the kitchen. And Logan and I weren't acting sketchy on purpose. I came up with a plan. Poppy always came into the kitchen to make a martini at six o'clock every night except Wednesday. But this cocktail hour would be different. I left the green earring on the kitchen counter as a trap. Taking it would prove Poppy wasn't the nice suburban girl next door she claimed to be.

"It has to." My eyes remained on Logan for a beat. Sure. He was lucky to have only a couple of scrapes on his chin and forehead. Although being his boyfriend meant breathing faster when danger even thought about flirting with Logan.

"I'd just like to know who cut my brakes," he mumbled. "Imagine if I needed more than stitches."

He didn't misspeak. The police determined the cut brakes caused his accident.

Footsteps pounded against the ground, and I put my

finger to my lips, making a shushing gesture. A bead of sweat dripped down my face. However, I had to vanquish my anxiety. Logan was with me, which meant there was nothing to fear if Poppy discovered us. Like that time Grandma knowingly took me to see an R-rated movie when I was thirteen without telling my parent. Because I wouldn't have gotten in trouble since I was with an adult.

More footsteps soon pounded on the ground again until growing fainter. Logan and I waited several moments before seeing if Poppy fell for the trap.

Over analyzing situations could be problematic. But Poppy could have realized I set her up and only pretended to sneak out of the kitchen before running back in. She might have even yelled surprise her after twisting my plan.

Wow. My plan worked. The earring was no longer on the kitchen counter. But the martini glass, and bottles of gin and vermouth were. So much for cocktail hour. She must have temporarily lost her thirst for booze. Like that time four years ago when Grandma couldn't have Gin and Tonics for a month because of some crash diet. Because that had to have been the most miserable month of her life. Gin was like a lifejacket to her, and there was no way she would have made it another day without gin. Sure. Some people might have chastised me for being so blunt about Grandma. But dwelling on a humorous story was much better than the alternative. Because I so wanted to obsess over how there was a good a chance I lived under the same roof as a murderer.

CHAPTER 37

Someone knocked on my bedroom door several after-noons later while I was in the middle of doing homework at my desk. I didn't even have a reason for an increased heartbeat. There was a good chance Poppy wouldn't have knocked. Being courteous wasn't something she would do. It wasn't like I could have my memory erased and forget how she took the earring from the kitchen counter. Like the time Grandma wanted her mind erased when she arrived half an hour late to an acquisition's meeting. Everyone in the room stared at her for what must have been the longest second of her life before she sat down.

"Come in," I said.

The door opened.

Wow. Maybe I was psychic. Placing a bet on who wanted to talk would have made me rich. Because Poppy didn't want to chat; Theresa did. And her face was all red in addition to her mascara stained eyelids. She also clenched her right hand, which had a tissue sticking out of it. Although that was a matter of semantics. I knew better than to jump conclusions. I was here if Theresa needed to talk, but I shouldn't have assumed something was true. Doing so would only embarrass myself.

My gaze narrowed. "I thought you had the fashion competition and weren't going to be home till later?"

I stood by my original opinion regarding not wanting to make assumptions about Theresa's current mood. However, I could guide the conversation since that action might make it easier for Theresa to tell me what troubled her.

"My designs were trashed," she said.

"Huh?"

"My dresses had stains and tears on them when the models walked onto the runway."

I drew in a breath. "When was the last time you looked at your dresses?"

"Last night."

"Where were they?" I asked.

"I left the garment bag in the television room."

Ding. Ding. Ding. Another million dollars for having a good intuition. Kidding. I didn't want Theresa to confirm my possible suspicion. Yet she had, and there was nothing wrong with making a guess. Nothing would ever get done in the world if people didn't make an occasional inference. Enough tangents, though. I had a good idea of who sabotaged her, and I couldn't lose sight of my suspicion.

She ran her fingers through her hair. "It's so awful, Casey. It's not like I thought I was entitled to win. I just wanted a chance."

"I understand."

Her gaze met mine. But she didn't respond, and I couldn't fault her for remaining silent. I would have been furious if someone sabotaged a writing opportunity for me. Like that time Grandma came home flabbergasted after discovering someone ate her yogurt that she kept in the company fridge despite how her name was written on it.

She glared. "Do you know something?"

"Just a theory."

"You have to tell me."

"There's no way to know for sure if I'm right."

"It doesn't matter. I deserve to know the truth," Theresa said.

"Of course."

"Do you know something, or not?" She put her hands on her hips. Great. Her gesture was just what I needed to skip down the street, whistling.

I lowered my gaze. "It's complicated."

"You have to tell me," she said.

Perfect. I so wanted to be put in a difficult situation, which was further proof of the universe always being on my side. Because it always made my life so easy.

"I can't," I said.

She stomped her feet. "What do you mean? If you cared about me, then you'd reveal the truth."

This conversation was the one time I wouldn't criticize Theresa for acting bratty. Doing so would have been unfair. Theresa had a right to feel whatever she felt. There was also a chance that being critical would have been made her angrier.

There was enough rage glowing in her eyes to last several lifetimes. Theresa probably wouldn't have a spring in her step for several weeks.

"You have to tell me the truth." Theresa grunted. "My designs weren't even scored; I was just asked to leave."

Shit. Theresa was smarter than I realized since she wouldn't forget about me having something important to tell her. Damn. I had to make a decision fast. Although I couldn't help myself. Both possibilities were fair. I understood how she would want to know the truth in addition to how protecting her from knowing Poppy's true cruelty. But real life still wasn't like the German movie *Run, Lola, Run,* which meant I couldn't freeze everyone and try a new outcome.

"I'm waiting," Theresa said.

She deserved credit for one thing. Her hands hadn't left her hips. But going off on another ramble wouldn't change how I had a decision to make. I could think of how she would have won some sort of award for the longest amount of time for putting her hands on her hips later.

"Get Sadie and Tony, and I'll get Logan," I said.

"What do they have to do with my sabotage dresses?"

"You'll find out soon."

Theresa winced. "This isn't a game."

"I never said it was. I just think we should all be here together."

"What if Tony and Sadie say they're busy?" She crushed the tissue harsher. Damn. Poor girl. The lousy day must have gotten to her more than either one of us realized. I never saw someone crush a tissue so intensely before. It wasn't like the tissue did anything to her.

"Tell them it's an emergency," I said.

***

"What is so important that Sadie and I couldn't have our date?" Tony asked sometime later while he, Theresa, Sadie, and Logan stood in my bedroom near my desk.

Logan glanced at me. "Are you doing what I think you're doing?"

I nodded. "There's no other way."

I paused for a beat, letting myself take in another breath. One. Two. Three. Everything would be okay. It just had to be. "Logan and I think Poppy killed Grandma and the daughter she gave up for adoption."

CHAPTER 38

"What you're saying is crazy," Tony said once I finished unloading on him, Theresa, and Sadie, while Logan stood next to me.

Logan bit his lip. "This isn't something Casey wants to be right about."

Logan's defense was what I needed. Sure. I was capable of advocating for myself, but there was a reason I wanted Logan here too. And his presence wasn't just because he was nice to stare at. He was also good moral support since the Poppy situation was more than I should have dealt with at my age.

"I've been waffling for a long time," I said.

Sadie shifted her gaze toward me. "Why didn't you say anything sooner? I could have helped you."

Someone might have gotten annoyed with Sadie if the person was in my position, but I couldn't fret. She just acted like a mamma bear. Being the same age didn't stop her from protecting me. Like the first time we met in the first grade when a playground bully stole my iPhone and Sadie demanded he give it back to me.

"Forget it. The question was stupid," Sadie continued.

Logan rubbed his forehead. "It's not like we can go to the police. We just know a bunch of little things."

Theresa grimaced. "It's more than a bunch of little things. Uncle Brad lied when he gave her an alibi, the inn receptionist let her into Violet's room, Uncle Brad's gun went missing, Logan's mom saw her acting unhinged before going in the car and driving somewhere, Violet's ex-husband recanted even though he was Violet's legitimate alibi. And we can't forget about Poppy's earring being under Grandma's bed and Poppy taking it when finding it in the kitchen. There's also the fact Poppy sent Grandma the nasty email. Plus, Casey saw her stalking him a few times, like outside the gallery window. But I haven't even gotten to the best part. Poppy's affair with Uncle Brad. And there's also my designs. I guess she wanted to show Casey that there are consequences to his actions. No offense, Casey."

"None taken," I said.

Tony let out a nervous laugh. "My head is spinning."

"Mine isn't," Theresa said.

Tony glanced at his sister. "You always assume the worst in people."

"I'm not assuming the worst in her if it's true," Theresa said.

Sadie sneered. "I'm not surprised."

"You aren't?" I asked.

Sadie straightened her long-sleeved blouse's collar. "Nope. There was always something off about Poppy."

"You should have told me," I said.

Sadie shook her head while remaining silent.

"Anyway, I hope I did the right thing by telling the truth," I continued.

Being consumed with worry about whether telling Theresa was the right thing to do or not couldn't be helped. Knowing the truth was ultimately a burden. Theresa would have never known the truth if her dresses weren't ruined, and she could have gone on living life with all the springs in her steps she wanted.

Theresa nodded. "You did."

Sadie played with a strand of her hair. "Cutting the car brakes and trying to strangle you crosses a line. We need to go to the police."

"We have no forensic evidence," I said.

"You have the earring," Sadie said.

I forced in a breath. "The police could say I planted it to make Poppy look guilty."

Logan's mouth gaped. "I didn't even think about that."

"Do you think she took Violet's letter to Grandma?" Theresa asked me.

"Maybe."

Theresa's question was simple enough, but I hadn't given Violet's missing letter much thought since discovering it was gone. My mind was too full with every other dramatic thing that happened to be worried about one more problem. The scary thing was how stealing the letter was minor in the grand scheme of things. The two murders were what made sweat always trickle out of my pores in addition to how I always had to kept checking my surroundings to make sure I wasn't about to be attacked.

Tony pursed his lips. "It's circumstantial at best."

"Why do you want to give Poppy the benefit of the doubt?" Theresa demanded.

"She's family," Tony replied.

"That doesn't mean we have to enable her homicidal tendencies," Theresa said.

Sadie's face drooped. "I'm sorry, Tony, but I'm with Theresa. Your safety is now at risk."

Theresa huffed. "I'll prove the truth to you if you don't believe me."

Tony sneered. "You're just pissed you lost the competition."

Even I wasn't stupid enough to be callous. He was also her brother, and should have known better than to make a silly statement. Theresa had every right for rage to flicker through her body. Theresa had never done anything bad to Poppy and was only collateral damage. And there was no problem with making a logical leap. People made snapped judgements all the time in life. The only difference with me was how I wasn't doing something impulsive based on my opinion.

"I bet Poppy has Violet's letter." Theresa darted out of my bedroom without another word. Not that I should have been surprised. Having a clear "mission" meant vindicating her concerns.

"We should follow her," I said.

"Poppy's still at work," Tony said.

Sadie gave her boyfriend a dirty look. "No offense or anything, but man up. Being flimsy isn't sexy."

Yuck. Sexy wasn't something Sadie should have said in front of me. Like the time Grandma used the word sexy when she took me out for Chinese food last March and she spotted a hot man.

Now wasn't the time to debate proper etiquette, though. Not when there was a slim chance Poppy could have discovered Theresa in her bedroom. Because I would have hated to see what happened next.

Thinking Poppy could discover Theresa in her bedroom wasn't illogical. She did sometimes come home from work early. And I now knew why Uncle Brad put up with that fact. But I would never be okay with wrapping around my head around Uncle Brad and Poppy's affair. Common sense meant giving brief consideration about how he was her stepfather.

"You shouldn't be in here, Theresa," I said after entering Poppy's bedroom.

Theresa held a letter in one hand, and a stationery pad in another.

I squinted. The stationery wasn't some random paper with roses on the perimeter. Because I would have recognized the stationery anywhere as a result of the roses being black. Like when Grandma could tell if it would be a good or bad day from the second she woke up in the morning.

But we still weren't any closer with getting out of Poppy's bedroom. And that meant impressing upon Theresa about the seriousness of getting out of here ASAP.

"Casey's right. Let's get out of here," Tony said after he, Logan, and Sadie trekked into Poppy's room.

"We now know Poppy took Violet's letter," Theresa said. "It's not like it could walk away by itself."

"Fine." Tony exhaled a breath. "But why would she need Violet's letter?"

"To forge a suicide note," Sadie said.

"You're making a lot of assumptions," Tony said.

The shuffling of footsteps echoed before the bedroom door's lock clinked. But we were too involved in the conversation for our back hairs to rise or to be overcome with dread.

Someone cackled. "Don't be so cynical. The assumptions are true."

Our attention shifted. Poppy stood in front of her locked bedroom door. Although I didn't even care about her finding us snooping in her bedroom. The sparkle from the metal object she gripped and pointed at us caused the dry feeling in my throat. There was just no nice way to mention Poppy had us at gunpoint. Like when Grandma once fell out of bed and injured her hip, which made her drop the F-bomb. Because a spade sometimes needed to be called a spade.

CHAPTER 39

My throat tightened even more. Poppy couldn't have walked into her bedroom with a gun. This just couldn't be my life. Stringing every clue together was one thing, but having my worst fear confirmed was another thing altogether. She was supposed to be my family; not a killer.

But maybe, just maybe, I could work Poppy's appearance to my advantage. I moved a little so that Logan slightly blocked Poppy's view of me. Then, I pulled out my iPhone and turned it on.

Poppy's nostrils flared. "You're wasting my time."

"You really killed Grandma, didn't you?" I asked after pulling up an app and pressing something before putting my iPhone back in my pocket.

Poppy inched closer while her hands remained on the trigger. "You should know better than to ask a silly question. Although I should thank you for finding my earring."

Logan stepped in front of me. Tony did the same for Sadie while Theresa remained to my right. I would have even taken a minute to appreciate Logan's chivalry with defending me. But Poppy still had the gun pointed at us, and we needed to figure out what to ASAP so we could survive.

My jaw trembled. "You could at least tell us the truth if you're going to kill us."

Listening to a villain monologue wasn't ideal. Getting Poppy talking would bide us time we needed, though. Sure. Poppy outwitting the entire family revealed she was smart. But having Poppy revel in her victory revealed I was just as cunning. I would find a way out of the situation; I just had to. Like the time Grandma got a flat tire in a rural part of California after attending a writer's conference. Her cellphone battery died and she waited for over an hour for another car to pass by to help her.

And not attacking her didn't make us dumb. It made us practical. Angering someone holding a gun was the last thing anyone of us wanted to do.

Poppy smirked. "I guess we have a few minutes. Because I would hate for people to think I'm cruel by denying you your last request."

"You didn't answer my question," I said, stuttering.

Tony gave me a dirty look. Okay. Fine. Nobody else wasn't charging up to her. But we weren't thinking the exact same thing. Tony wouldn't have focused on melting with his gaze if we were.

"Did Grandma know you flunked out of college?" I asked.

Poppy gave me a mock frown. "I thought you could keep a secret?"

"Answer his question," Logan said.

"She found out about my affair with Brad and was gonna tell mom unless I told her first," Poppy said.

"How did the affair with Uncle Brad start in the first place?" I asked.

"I was distraught one night after my fall semester last year and one thing led to another." She paused for a second. "He was the one who came up with the idea of me working for him so mom wouldn't get suspicious."

My eyes widened. "Did you strangle me?"

Yes. I could have made an assumption and guessed Poppy tried to kill me, but she had to admit the truth. Poppy couldn't be as terrible as she seemed. Even if her gun continued facing us. My life just couldn't be like some horror ripped from the eleven o'clock news. That was Grandma's domain when she was alive; not mine.

"I wasn't trying to kill you," Poppy said. "I was just trying to scare you."

Please. She shouldn't have insulted my intelligence. My throat closing off from all the pressure she applied when strangling sure felt real.

"What about the day at the inn?" I asked.

"I wasn't stalking you that day. I had an impromptu afternoon tryst with Brad. What about you five? How did you find out my affair?" Poppy inched forward, making the rest of us step back.

Great. As if the situation wasn't tense enough. We so needed our pulses to soar faster.

Although what Poppy didn't say revealed the bigger truth. Incorporating the phrase, "that day" hinted she might have stalked me and really have been standing outside the gallery the night of Sadie's art debut in addition to when Logan and I went to the park to meet with Violet's ex-husband.

"Logan and I followed you on Wednesday night. Althhough it was pretty risky of you to kiss Uncle Brad," I said.

Poppy's face turned bright red. And I even laughed. I hadn't realized she was capable of getting flustered. Apparently, people learn something new every day.

"What about Violet?" I asked.

"She only has herself to blame. I wasn't going to frame her until I stumbled upon their conversation. The stupid bitch delayed my plan to kill Grandma." Poppy took one hand off the trigger and wiped a bead of sweat from her face. "Although I did the right thing. I made it look like I was looking for something in the hallway and didn't enter Grandma's bedroom until Violet was long gone."

My eyes almost rolled out of my head.

"Although you should have hidden her letter better. You made the whole thing way easier than it should have been," Poppy said.

Great. She provided me with an answer to a question I hadn't asked, but I wouldn't complain. Every second that went by was one more second that we had to live. And I still hadn't figured out what to do about Poppy pointing a gun at us.

Perhaps placing the entire burden on myself was unfair, though. There were four other people who should have been trying to come up with a plan. Because I wouldn't have argued with getting some help.

"Does Uncle Brad know?" I asked.

"No. But he's suspicious," Poppy said.

"How so?" Sadie asked.

Wow. Sadie said something. Because she might as well have not been in the bedroom. She usually made her voice heard. Like back in my bedroom when she didn't hesitate to criticize Tony over his waffling.

"He's grown distant. But enough talking. Get ready to meet your maker," Poppy said.

"Wait," Logan said. "How did you even know we were in your bedroom? Do you have the mansion bugged?"

Thank goodness for Logan. Time was up, and I hadn't come up with an idea. But everything would be fine since Logan bought us more time. Like when Grandma succeeded with convincing a bank to give her one more month to pay back her business loan when I was three years old. Only an idiot would have been oblivious to how Grandma and money was a great combination.

Poppy snorted. "No, you fool. I happened to overhear

you talking as I was about enter my bedroom, and went to Uncle Brad's safe and borrowed another one of his guns."

"You can't kill us," I blurted.

Poppy cocked her eyebrows. "Why the hell not?"

"You'll never get away with it. One of us, maybe. But not five. It'd raise too many questions. Surely, you're smart enough to realize that," I replied.

She beamed her eyes. "What are you suggesting?"

"We won't tell anyone what we know if you let us live. It'll be like the whole thing never happened," I said.

"Forgetting" about what we knew might not have been the best plan. But the idea was the only one I had. There was also a difference between losing a battle and winning a war, and I would just have to hope I would get justice for Grandma someday.

"What's to stop you guys from ratting me out the second you leave my bedroom?" Poppy asked.

"Our fear of you should be obvious at this point," I said.

Poppy just stared at me for the longest before grunting. "Deal. But let's get one thing clear. I'll turn the tables on you, Casey, if you or the others rat me out."

I scoffed. "And how would you do that?"

"By going to the police and concoct some story about you and Grandma fighting in the weeks leading up to her death," Poppy said. "I could even steal one of your hairs from your comb and plant it in Grandma's bedroom before suggesting the police go through her room again."

"Seriously?" I asked.

My opinion of Poppy might have plummeted faster than it took Grandma to get ready for a party. However, even I needed to be pinched. Staging a crime scene was something I expected an experienced criminal to do, begging the question of just how evil Poppy was.

"Yes," Poppy said. "I need an insurance policy."

I grunted. "Fine. We have a deal. Although excuse me if I don't shake your hand."

"The feeling is mutual," Poppy said.

Sassing Poppy might not have accomplished much, but I needed any victory I could get. My earlier point remained true since I had to get justice for Grandma's murder. At least in a small way. And if insulting Poppy accomplished that goal, then so be it. Although I could still have my fantasy about Poppy being arrested and going to jail for Grandma's murder for a fleeting moment. Because I didn't need to be a kid to appreciate how heroes should have triumphed over villains in real life just like in Disney movies. Even if Grandma would have lectured me about being smart enough to know life wasn't fair.

CHAPTER 40

Logan and I sat at one of the tables in the high school library the next morning before first period. And I would have grinned about going to the library if I wasn't dealing with the Poppy situation. Because I could count the amount of times I went to the library over the last two years on one hand. Something intimidating just existed about being here. And my opinion was more than about the stern look the head librarian gave when people talked too loudly. There was more to life than checking out reference books, using online databases, and learning how to cite a source in MLA format.

Although I couldn't further contemplate the irony of a writer hating the library. Because forget about Mrs. Baker's constant venomous glare. Logan had given me a look of his own. Although there was no need to have an increased pulse yet. Logan was my boyfriend, and I needed to listen to what he had to say first.

"You aren't even focusing on your last problem," Logan said.

"I can't help it," I mumbled.

"Did you sleep at all last night?"

"No offense, but that's a loaded question."

He leaned closer. "Do you feel unsafe in your own house?"

I shrugged. "I don't know."

He grabbed my hand. "I'm sorry about your situation."

"Thank you. I appreciate it."

Mrs. Baker blew a lock of her hair out of the way before standing. She strutted away from the checkup desk and started to pick up her pace. I would have even made a comment about her getting sores on her feet from moving so fast if I wasn't preoccupied. But there was no time for my inner commentary when she was several inches away from the table Logan and I sat at.

Damn. Sitting at the front table was a mistake. Yet Logan and I hadn't a choice. All the other tables were full.

Wait. Mrs. Baker wasn't fuming about Logan and I making excessive noise. She already passed by our table, and now stood in front of the table behind Logan and I. She whispered something to the girls and guys at the table, who must have been freshman as a result of their short stature. The group rose and tossed everything into their backpacks before flocking out of the library.

Mrs. Baker even smirked while she rubbed her hair, which was wrapped in a bun. Damn. I was so preoccupied with my worries and keeping up with my conversation with Logan that I hadn't realized the group that just left had been talking loudly. I should have also been concerned about Mrs. Baker getting pleasure in kicking the students out. But I was yawning too much for my brain to operate at full capacity.

Yup. I hadn't gotten much sleep last night as a result of worrying about Poppy sneaking into my room and slitting my throat the second I closed my eyes. Shit. I was pretty sure Logan would give me another evil eye. He was speaking, yet I had no idea what he was saying.

He gave me a small smile. "Just know I'm always here for you no matter what."

"Same."

***

Irony wouldn't escape my life anytime soon.

Yup. Another ironic thing happened hours later after being in the library. Mom, Dad, Uncle Brad, and Aunt Rita weren't in the mood to go to the Founder's Day party at the Redwood Mansion in town on Main Street, yet Mom insisted on Theresa, Tony, and I attend. And there was no arguing with her once she had her mind made up. Because that's where Theresa, Tony, Sadie, Logan, and I were since we just walked into the lobby.

A waiter walked up to us. "Would you like some Champagne?"

The waiter wasn't bizarre for serving us. But I should have backed up and explained tonight's function more. The Redwood Mansion was private property, and was owned by the Redwood family, which was the oldest family in town. They threw this party every year as a way of appreciating the town. And Grandma would have approved if she were alive. There was nothing more that she liked than a good party. She even referred to last Christmas as a party when she asked if I had a good time.

"Thanks," I said, taking a Champagne flute from the tray.

Sadie, Tony, Theresa, and Logan followed my lead and helped themselves to Champagne too. The waiter then walked away as soon as he arrived.

One gaze around the room revealed the event would be a hit. The chattering of various people in tuxedoes and cocktail dresses echoed through the lobby.

Sadie giggled. "Maybe tonight wasn't a mistake. We need a break."

"Where's Poppy?" Logan asked.

"She had to finish up a few things at work." I finished my Champagne. Yet the mixture of the sweet and tart flavors and carbonation didn't excite my taste buds. The beverage just pricked my throat before trickling down into my stomach.

Logan patted my shoulder. "I'm sorry. I shouldn't have mentioned Poppy."

I sighed. "Don't worry about it."

Being the bigger person wasn't about making excuses for Logan since he was my boyfriend. I just didn't want to talk about Poppy. Because she wasn't a good person. There was no excusing killing Grandma. Real life wasn't a movie, and that meant never forgiving Poppy. Grandma even would have approved of my vindictiveness. She was the one who once skipped out on her bar tab because she was convinced the bartender used low quality gin in her Gin and Tonics.

"The important thing is that we're alive," Sadie said.

My stomach was tighter than the tightest knot. But I could take a minute to appreciate Sadie's dress. And my staring wasn't even because her cocktail dress was baby blue, which was my favorite color. My opinion encompassed more than her high heels or Gucci purse. Sadie spruced up her appearance because her hair was wavy tonight as opposed to its usual flat and straight texture.

"Boo," said someone.

We turned around at the same time.

Poppy just had to be here. She sported a mink coat and black dress, which extended to her ankles. I could have given her props for how she changed her look. Her hair was wavy like Sadie's in addition to her diamond belt, which twinkled because of being under an overhead light. But I wouldn't pay her any niceties—I would have rather shot myself in the foot than say kind thing about her. Like the time Grandma punched herself instead of admitting she lost a bet about who would win the 2016 US Presidential Election.

"Are you trying to give us a heart attack?" Theresa asked.

A creative writing snob might have criticized Theresa for being dramatic. But she had a point because of my already established opinion of being unwilling to do one nice for thing for Poppy. Now just wasn't the time to mince words. Not when a serial killer stood in my presence.

Wait. Serial killer might not have been accurate phrase. Poppy only killed two people.

Fuck. I didn't need a label to tell me Poppy was a bad person. I just had to trust my intuition. Because the achy feeling jolting my body as a result of Poppy was worse than when there was a change in the barometric pressure.

"Maybe," Poppy said, then smiled. "I was just making conversation."

"It wasn't appreciated," Sadie said.

"Can't you talk to anyone else? There are a bunch of other people here?" Logan's eyes dilated, making their blue color more distinct and menacing.

Poppy cackled. "You should control your boyfriend, Casey. I would hate for anything to happen to him."

Hold on. Poppy couldn't have said what she just did. If I didn't know better, I would have thought she just threatened my boyfriend.

"Don't fuck with us, bitch, because we made a deal. Or maybe you don't know what mutually assured destruction is," I said.

Poppy's lips curled. "I know what the word means."

"Then back off," I said. "Because I recorded everything you said yesterday and emailed it to several different email accounts I created."

Poppy hissed. "You did what?"

Yeah. I didn't just have Poppy talk up a storm to bide us more time. I recorded everything she said. And I hadn't dwelled on the fact because too much fear trembled through my body when doing it from thinking Poppy would get even angrier. Even if Poppy needed to know I recorded her so she realized I wasn't weak.

Poppy gripped the sides of her fur coat. "I won't make a scene because this is a public party. But just remember I'm always watching you because we live in the same house. Besides, don't forget about our deal, and how I could point the police in your direction if I wanted to."

Poppy could make all the threats she wanted, but she wouldn't make us flinch. At least in front of her. Sadie, Tony, Theresa, Logan, and I were winning "the game." Poppy hadn't succeeded with killing us, and that was enough to hold onto. Or at least I thought it was. Maybe if I believed my pulse could slow down, then it actually would. It wasn't like I could go to the police with my recording. Poppy wasn't just some random person from a poor neighborhood people would forget about it. She was a white girl from a wealthy family. So, she could make bail. Or worse. Get acquitted.

CHAPTER 41

Sadie, Tony, Theresa, Logan, and I met the following morning in one of the school hallways on the second floor. I sent everyone a text, insisting we needed to talk before first period, and they might as well never talk to me again if they didn't show.

Kidding. I would never type something so nasty into a text unless addressed to Poppy. But my exaggeration communicated the urgency of today's meeting. Like when Mom once lied about an event's start time so Grandma wouldn't be late.

Sadie played with a strand of her hair. "Is everything okay, Casey?"

I coughed, clearing the scratchiness from my throat. Yet no amount of stalling would change what needed to be said. This was real life, and I couldn't wish away my problems.

"Out with it," Theresa said.

I cracked my knuckles. "I'm going to the police after school today to turn Poppy in."

"Do you think your recording will be enough?" Sadie asked.

"I have to try. I mean, you were there with me at the Founder's Day party. We can't just pretend nothing is wrong for the rest of our lives," I said.

"We made a deal with Poppy," Tony said.

Logan drew in a breath. "And what about Poppy's threat?"

"It's a risk I have to take," I said.

My response was true even if Grandma would have smacked me for risking my future. Poppy had to be stopped. She killed Grandma, and that wasn't okay.

So, yeah. The situation wouldn't end until I did something about it.

Theresa snorted. "That's noble of you."

Having patience with Theresa was best. She might not have talked about it anymore, but losing the fashion competition took a toll on her. Theresa hadn't drawn in her fashion sketchbook in days. Because I would have still been pissed off if I were Theresa. Sabotaging a career interest was personal.

Logan's Adam's apple throbbed. "Positive you wanna do this?"

Good for Logan. He hadn't used his response as a way to hear himself talk. He just wanted to make sure I could live with my choice. Because that type of behavior guaranteed Logan a perfect boyfriend trophy — if such a thing existed.

"Yes," I said.

"Then why consult us if you made up your mind?" Theresa asked.

"I'm not the only involved in this situation," I said.

I couldn't forget about Sadie, Theresa, Tony, and Logan. Poppy might have only threatened to make me a suspect in Grandma's murder, but she was still unhinged, which meant being on the lookout for possible surprises. I so loved surprises.

Sadie gave me a weak smile. "If you think going to the police is the right thing to do, then you should."

"Agreed," Tony added.

Theresa giggled. "You already know how I feel about Poppy."

I turned to Logan.

"I just want you to be happy." Logan squeezed my shoulder. "And I'm happy to go with you to back you up. Or if you feel like you need to do this alone, then that's cool too."

"Then it's decided," I said. "I'm going to go to the police after school. Consequences be damned."

The bell screeched before anyone could respond, yet life was fine. I made my decision, and would stick to it. Doing so was the right thing to do. Instance justice might have been naïve, but I would never forgive myself if Poppy got away with Grandma's murder.

***

"So, what do you think? Will you be able to use the recording?" I asked, gripping my coffee cup hours later, as I sat in Detective Johnson's office afterschool. I just showed her the recording, and couldn't contain my squealing about Poppy maybe going to jail.

Yup. I hadn't misspoken, and had no qualms about drinking more coffee. Because I would have rather gone to school for all of summer than turn down free coffee. However, it would have been nice if the steam stopped seeping from the chipped mug. Coffee was supposed to be consumed, not admired.

"Absolutely." She leaned her elbows onto the table. Although now wasn't the time to snicker about Grandma's incessant belief in manners. My ramble could wait till later since I had to see my mission through.

"Good, because I would hate to think Poppy would get away with what she did." My eyes drifted around the office, yet I scowled. Detective Johnson didn't have any family photos on her wooden desk or bookshelf to the left of her chair. No specs of dust covered her desk in addition to how it also didn't contain one misplaced file or piece of paper. The writer in me would have thought she was too perfect. Like with how Grandma said she didn't trust people that voted Republican. Something about politics revealing a person's greater morality compass — or lack thereof.

"The best thing to do would be to try and get her to confess," Detective Johnson said. "Anyway, I admire the poise you carry yourself with despite what you've been through. Because you certainly are no longer the terrified boy I interviewed the night of your Grandma's murder."

Grandma might have turned her nose up at unexpected praise, but I didn't dissect Detective Johnson's comment. I just needed to be done. Having a "normal" life—or at least an attempt at one—was the least I deserved after all the dramatic events since Poppy killed Grandma.

***

I entered my family's mansion sometime later, only to bump into Poppy, who just walked out of the kitchen. Contempt radiated from her eyes as a result of her narrow gaze. Yet I couldn't think of Poppy going to the dark side. Doing so would only make my stomach burn more.

She crossed her arms. "I got an interesting call today."

"Really?"

I might not have been a genius, but playing dumb was essential. Poppy couldn't think I backstabbed her. Not even for a second. Because I was more than aware of what she did to people who fucked with her.

A detective wants to be speak to me," Poppy said. "Something about unresolved questions about Grandma's death. But she assures me I'm not in trouble."

"That's good." My heart fluttered, yet I couldn't waver. So far, so good. Unless Poppy wanted to choose her battles carefully.

She pouted. "If you say so."

"I'm sure it's nothing. You even said you aren't in trouble."

"Yeah."

"I should go do homework," I said before walking towards the stairwell.

Poppy grabbed my arm, making me almost recoil. "You didn't rat me out to the police, did you?"

"Even I'm not that stupid."

"Great." Poppy paused for the longest time. "Because I'd hate for anything to happen to Logan."

I couldn't swallow the lump in my throat. "Same."

CHAPTER 42

"Thanks for coming over," I said after Logan and I sat down on my bed a few minutes after Poppy left for the police station

"No problem."

A silence ensued even though neither one of us said anything bad. I just couldn't help having my pulse drum in my ears. Going to the police, Poppy getting the call and then rushing off to meet with Detective Johnson actually happened. So, there was no undoing what I did, and I hoped nothing bad would happen. Silencing the inner cynic in me also took all the strength I had. There were a bunch of different ways my plan could wrong and not considering them was next to impossible. Even if I warned Detective Johnson Poppy might point a finger at me.

Logan stared at me. "I'm in awe of you."

"Excuse me?"

"I'm serious. What you did took guts, and I've never been prouder to call you my boyfriend."

"I didn't go to the police station so you would praise me," I said.

He shook his head. "I don't care. It needed to be said."

"What do you think will happen?" I fanned myself with my T-shirt. Yeah. I couldn't escape sweat oozing out of every pore in my body even though it was fall.

"It doesn't matter. You aren't in this alone."

I lifted my gaze off my carpet. "You always know the right thing to say."

"It's my job."

We continued making eye contact with each other while my blood pumped faster through my veins. Logan extended an arm and pushed a lock of my hair out of the way before kissing me. His hand traveled to each of my cheeks while we continued our embrace. The mixture of his deodorant's sweet and earthly smell wafted through the air, and drifted to my nostrils before I inhaled the scent, and kissed Logan with more vigor. And I would have laughed at myself six months ago if someone told me I would have a boyfriend and be engage in a passionate lip lock, yet I was only human. So, I didn't even blink when Logan's hands traveled to my stomach and lifted my shirt over my head and tossed it aside. Although he pulled back after another beat.

I raised my eyebrows. "What's wrong?"

"We should talk."

"I'm not a kid. I know what sex is," I said.

He chuckled. "I know, but I want to make sure you want to do this."

I threw a gaze at my desk drawer. "I'm prepared."

"Great. But we still haven't figured out the most important thing."

I winked. "And what's that?"

"I think you know what I'm talking about."

"You're right. I just wanted you to sweat for a sec."

"We need to figure out the specifics."

"It's kind of obvious," I said. "Besides, my parents, Aunt Rita, and Uncle Brad have some publishing function to attend, and we thus should take advantage of not having any interruptions."

He beamed his eyes. "Really? Then why don't you enlighten me?"

"Less thinking, more kissing." I pulled Logan in for another kiss, then wrapped my hands around his cheeks this time. Our heads both thudded onto my pillow and we continued making out.

A part of me might have had some idolized idea about what my first time with Logan would be like, but I didn't need perfection. Knowing I had a kind boyfriend provided enough comfort. My opinion went back to something Grandma once said about ideas only being flawless in someone's head because they would get muddied with imperfection once executed. Mentioning Grandma right as Logan and I were about to be intimate wasn't sexy, though. I also needed to silence the inner cynic in me. The details of what was about to transpire with Logan would stay between the two of us. Like my first time with him was our only little secret. Because even I appreciated the cheesy expression about it not being polite to kiss and tell.

***

I grabbed two water bottles from the kitchen fridge hours later while donning my bathrobe, only to gasp when turning around.

"Everything okay, Uncle Brad?" I asked. "I thought you were supposed to go to that function tonight?"

"Poppy called me from the police station."

"Okay,"

"Don't act so innocent. She knows you ratted her out," he revealed.

So much for hoping I fooled Poppy. I should have known better than to think my plan would be perfect. The universe never hesitated to turn the screws on me, and tonight was no exception. Like when Grandma once had the misfortunate of getting five red lights in me. There was no letting something like that go. She bitched about that event

212

for a good hour before shutting up and making a Gin and Tonic.

I cackled. "Why did she call you? You aren't a lawyer."

"Duh. She needs me to find a lawyer."

"Don't you care about what Poppy did?"

"The only thing that's important is how Poppy's actions prove she loves me."

"You two really do deserve each other," I said.

Yeah. I had no misgivings about insulting Uncle Brad and Poppy. Somebody needed to call them out for their relationship, and it might as well have been. Because a label wasn't necessary to realize they were both bad news.

Uncle Brad's eyes traveled to my bathrobe. "I hope you enjoyed your sexy time with your boyfriend—your days are numbered."

"What's that supposed to mean?" I tied my bathrobe tighter. Great. Having Uncle Brad make a colorful remark would make me smile 24/7. I so needed him to comment on my love life. Please. As if it was any of his business.

"Poppy knows how to play the long game and she'll come for you one day," Uncle Brad said.

"Is your threat supposed to scare me?" I asked.

"It's not a threat. It's a fact."

"Aren't you curious about how Aunt Rita will react?"

He picked his nail. "Things have a way of working themselves out."

Interesting. He hadn't even flinched. Because I would have been pacing back and forth if I were Uncle Brad. Something about Grandma engraining in me I couldn't be as careless as her "idol"—former president Bill Clinton.

"Poppy didn't try to pin this on me?" I asked.

Contemplating Poppy's threat didn't make me foolish. It made me practical. I couldn't snap my fingers and forget the day in Poppy's bedroom when she pointed her gun at me and everyone else. That type of event would haunt me till my last breath. Something about drama being more entertaining to watch on TV than witness firsthand.

Uncle Brad bit his lips. "No. Even she knows when something is a lost cause."

Footsteps echoed, making Uncle Brad and I look up.

Logan entered the kitchen, and he still sported his same white T-shirt and plaid boxers he slipped back into when I left to get the water bottles. Yet I needed to swoon over my boyfriend since my tongue would always wet my lips whether he sported clothing or not. Although I should have taken a minute to appreciate Logan's chivalry, because I could be both independent and not afraid to ask for help. In this moment, Logan was my golden ticket to freedom. I could only trade jabs with Uncle Brad for so long.

"I was worried about you," Logan said to me.

"I'm fine. But let's go back to my bedroom." I checked my hands. Great. I still held both water bottles, because I could never be too careful. Distraction only took one fleeting moment to take root in my mind.

Uncle Brad snickered. "I'm serious, gentlemen. The pendulum will swing the other way, and Poppy will be vindicated."

"Poppy was arrested?" Logan asked.

Waiting around for Uncle Brad's response would have been futile. I could fill in Logan later, and so I just threw my gaze towards the hallway, before Logan and I strutted away. Besides, life might not have been perfect, but I could at least attempt to have my first time with Logan be a picturesque moment. Because Uncle Brad's words contained a hint of truth regardless of me being loathed to admit so. Poppy might have been a lot of things, yet she wasn't dumb, and I couldn't imagine what she would do to me if our paths ever crossed again.

CHAPTER 43

Sadie, Theresa, Tony, and I stood by my locker the following morning at school.

Logan joined us a minute later, then furrowed his eyebrows. "What with the dark circles under your eyes?"

Sadie pointed to Theresa, Tony, and I. "These guys didn't get any sleep."

"What do you mean?" Logan asked.

"Aunt Rita threw Uncle Brad out of the mansion when her, and my parents returned form the function. But she didn't have the curtesy to do it before arguing," I revealed.

Logan gasped. "She knows?"

"Yup. Tony, Theresa, and my parents and I unwillingly got dragged into the longest night of our lives," I said.

"What about Poppy?" Logan asked.

"The police are holding her while they work out a plea bargain," I said, letting the lump linger in my throat.

Logan's shoulders shuddered. "You've gotta be kidding."

Theresa grunted. "Nope. Something about an insanity defense because of her mental deterioration after her college boyfriend broke up with her."

"That's bullshit," Logan said.

"No kidding," Theresa interrupted. "But that's what happens when someone gets the top-rated defense in the state."

Logan blinked. "How?"

"Uncle Brad knows Rene Ashley personally," Theresa said.

I pulled my backpack straps harder. "At least she's out of our lives."

Yeah. I hadn't misspoken. Every cell in my body might have burned with Poppy weaseling her way out of responsibility. But I didn't just need justice for Grandma; I needed her out of my life too. Because twisted was twisted. Poppy could rescue me from a burning building, and I would still give her the award for worst cousin of the year. Like with Grandma refusing to associate with Republicans.

Logan looped an arm around me. "Are you really okay?"

Being Logan's boyfriend was great and all. But I didn't need him to stare at me, and make me seem like his gaze would melt me.

"I'll be fine," I said.

Sadie clapped her hands together. "OMFG. You guys did it."

Fuck. Sadie raised her voice while she announced Logan and mine's news. Doing so would ensure I walked around skipping every second of the day.

"How can you tell?" Logan asked.

"I have a gift for that type of thing," Sadie said.

"How lucky for us," I said.

The fire alarm wailed. Great. Being outside was the place to be because I forgot to mention the rain pattering the ground since it had been a monsoon from the time I took my morning shower.

"Don't think you're saved by the bell," Sadie said. "We can all walk out of the building together."

I rolled my eyes. "Wonderful."

Not overreacting too much was essential. I could tell the difference between Sadie and Poppy. Besides, a normal teasing moment surpassed someone taking his or her first breath after almost drowning. Friends were supposed to joke with one another, and that meant bordering on being too nosy. Like when Grandma used to ask about my love life when she was alive. I so loved her putting me on the spot.

***

I entered the living room after coming home from school, only to find my parents sitting down on the couch and glaring at me.

"Hi," I said.

"Good. You saved us the trouble of finding you and telling you that we need to chat." Dad sneezed, and reached for a tissue on the living room table.

My heart skipped a beat. Yup. Dad elevated my stress level because teens so loved adults telling them they wanted to talk.

Mom locked her fingers together. "We didn't want to stress you last night given how afraid we all were of something happening between Rita and Brad, but the moment passed."

I laughed. "What's your point?"

"We're so disappointed you shut us out and didn't tell us about the Poppy situation," Mom said.

Fuck it. Grandma's bluntness was sometimes okay. My parents might have been older than me, but I had a right to stand up for myself. Omitting information also wasn't a bad thing. I was no longer some naïve five-year-old who had a naïve view of the world. I was a teenager, and understood how fucked up events sometimes couldn't

217

be avoided.

I yelled. "You have no idea what my life has been like."

Dad tugged at the sides of his blazer. "We don't want to punish you. We just want to spend more time with you."

"Okay." My eyes drifted to the photograph of Grandma and I resting on the table while I fought back tears. Sure. The photo was from when Grandma and I went to Disney World a couple of years, yet I couldn't not want to crawl into a fetal position. Following the Poppy trail took away from the bigger issue of Grandma being dead. Because I would have to face that reality soon.

"And that's why we're gonna resume semi-regular family dinners, starting tonight. You can even call Logan up and ask if he wants to join us," Mom said.

So much for almost becoming unhinged myself. Thinking I was in trouble, only to not be in trouble was something the universe enjoyed doing. I would know. The universe always dumped on me. Like when a bird crapped on Grandma right as she was about to walk into a hotel for an important publishing function. Although a bird crapping on someone was good luck. So, maybe, just maybe, I would take a few deep breaths and silence the inner cynic in me. Or I could relax, and watch *Gossip Girl* if getting rid of my constant opinions was unrealistic.

CHAPTER 44

The wind howled, scattering the various leaves, which were brown than any other color, the following day after school while I stood in the cemetery near Main Street.

Visiting Grandma's tombstone might have been morbid. But I needed to spend some time with her, and her grave was the closest thing I could get to that. Although closure could have also been a motivating factor — saying my feelings might help me to let go of her death's unfairness at least a little. Because the plea bargain went through, and Poppy now resided at the Lois Lena Sanitarium on the outskirts of town.

"I'm so sorry, Grandma." Tears welled in my eye before rolling down my cheeks. "You didn't deserve this, and it sucks Poppy is getting off easy. Because I'll never get to introduce you to Logan, or have you see me graduate high school and college, or even get a book published."

The wind picked up more, and nipped my face before the cold air traveled into my lungs. Great. Summer's tragic end wasn't enough. Winter just had to be around the corner, because it was my favorite season.

"You might have been sixty, but you could have lived for another twenty to thirty something years, and it's not okay your life was cut short. Because it feels like you were never even alive." More tears fell down my face while I made two fists. Purging my feelings was anything but easy, yet I freed myself of intense emotions, and would maybe be able to not stay awake, staring at the ceiling all night long one at some point. A guy could dream. Doing so wasn't a crime. Like with how Grandma dreamed of taking me to Rome when I graduated from high school even though she hadn't cleared the idea with my parents.

Fuck. Rome was another thing I forgot about. I so needed to be reminded of another lost opportunity with Grandma.

"It's gonna be okay," someone said before placing a hand on my right shoulder.

I looked up. Logan stood right next to me, and I would probably start stuttering from the possibility of him hearing what I just said.

"How much did you hear?" I asked.

"Enough."

"What are you doing here? I mean, don't get me wrong. Seeing you is always great. But I needed to do this alone."

"We talked about the possibility of going to the movies, and I went over to your house when you didn't respond to my texts," he said.

I took out my iPhone from pocket with the hand I wasn't holding the bouquet of roses. Wow. I had two missed text messages, and I deserved lashes with a wet noodle. Grandma would have slapped me if she knew I was becoming forgetful. Something about the importance of always staying sharp.

"I'm sorry, but I don't feel like going to the movies." I kneeled and placed the bouquet of roses down in front of

Grandma's purse.

He nodded. "That's fine. But why don't we go to Starbucks? My treat."

"Sure."

He chuckled. "Great. Although I'm serious. Don't argue with me about wanting to pay for yours."

"I wouldn't dream of it."

Logan grabbed my hand before we scurried out of the cemetery. A small amount of glee even radiated from my brief smile. Picking up the pace was commendable because being in a cemetery too long meant life resembled a Tim Burton movie or Edgar Allen Poe short story. Especially when a saturated gray color permeated the clouds even though it was only the first week of October, and was thus too early for a gray November day. And I couldn't have that. I would never be a complete optimist, but I could grasp at moments of happiness.

I enjoyed spending time with Logan. And that was something the universe couldn't steal from me.

CHAPTER 45

Tony, Sadie, Theresa, Logan, and I sat at one of the tables in back of Spinderwood Delights a couple of weeks after I "visited" Grandma at the cemetery. We had just gotten two orders of mozzarella sticks, consisting of eight sticks on each plate. We each also had a strawberry lemonade in front of us. And I even flashed a small smile. Like when Grandma got over her IRS drama. I might have been a pessimist, but even I could rejoice every now and then. Life wouldn't always be perfect. However, there was nothing wrong with appreciating a quieter everyday moment in light of all the drama since Grandma's death.

Theresa grinned. "Thanks for including me even though Dave couldn't make it."

Sadie giggled. "Excluding you would be cruel."

"At least the fashion club worked out for you since you have a boyfriend now." I sipped some of the strawberry lemonade. The sweet taste of the strawberry and the sour taste from the lemonade stayed on my tongue for a beat. Yet my body shuddered. Yeah. There was a good chance I would never order the strawberry lemonade again since life was just too short for bad food and drinks. According to Grandma. Wait. I remembered the expression. Because Mom's face wouldn't have turned bright red if Grandma made a tame comment. Grandma applied the expression to sex—not food and drinks.

"That's not all I'm thankful for." Theresa patted my hand. "I wouldn't have gotten a second chance with Carrie Marshall if it wasn't for you."

"It was the least I could do," I said.

Yup. I spoke with the local designer that Poppy botched Theresa's opportunity with. The universe even ended up being in a giving mood that day. Carrie agreed to hire Theresa as her assistant without any hesitation or equivocation. And that meant at pretending to be thankful for the universe for one fleeting moment.

Theresa shook her head. "You didn't have to do that."

"You didn't deserve to be one of Poppy's casualties," I said.

Sadie clutched her seal pendant necklace. "You could say that again."

"I propose a toast," Tony said, raising his glass. "Cheers to always being friends."

"I'll toast to that," Sadie said.

Everyone clinked their glasses, including me. Although I didn't drink more of my strawberry lemonade. I didn't need to learn my lesson again, and I would order a diet soda when the waitress came back with our dinner.

I drew in a breath before speaking. "I don't want to jinx anything, but what if Uncle Brad wants revenge for Poppy being locked up in a mental institution?"

Theresa giggled. "Don't worry. Aunt Rita saved our asses."

"A ten-million-dollar divorce settlement will do that," Tony added.

"It's got to be the fastest divorce settlement in history," I said.

Sadie tapped her fingers on the table. "I can't believe she would give your uncle money considering he cheated on her."

"I do," Theresa said. "Some problems aren't worth it, and at least this way it keeps her out of the spotlight. Although it would have been nice if Aunt Rita took us to Paris with her."

Oops. I didn't mention how Aunt Rita went to Paris on a whim. Although I didn't blame her. Most people would have been mortified when finding out their child cheated on them with their spouse. Yet Logan and I didn't have to worry about that problem. Being carefree was the great thing about being in love as a teenager.

I chuckled. "You're right. I should find a hobby."

I looked around the restaurant. There were only a couple of other filled tables. But my mind moved beyond how busy the restaurant. My gaze froze when it stopped at the window. Uncle Brad stood outside the restaurant on the sidewalk.

Damn. Uncle Brad couldn't be standing outside. The universe was supposed to be on my side. Because I so wanted to be at war with the universe again.

I squinted. He was gone when I opened my eyes.

"Something wrong?" Logan asked.

I could be honest and ruin the evening, or I could lie. Being honest was nice since it sounded like a pure idea. But everything I had been through since Grandma's death proved life wasn't black and white. Uncle Brad's brief reappearance was like an ugly baby. It just wasn't polite to comment about a baby being ugly. The remark would only make the mom and dad's baby angry at the person who made the rude comment. And that was what the same thing that would happen if I mentioned Uncle Brad. He and Poppy were like cancer, and would be difficult to eradicate for good. There was even a strong possibility they would always lurk on the peripheral of my life until I took them down once and for all. Getting what I wanted wasn't always a simple task, and that meant I couldn't wave a wand and make Poppy and Uncle Brad not exist.

Yup. My choice was a no-brainer. Dinner was my opportunity to pretend my life was perfect. And that meant lying.

"No. I actually don't have any complaints for once," I said.

Burning Bridges
By Chris Bedell

They've always said that three's a crowd...

24-year-old Sasha didn't anticipate her identical twin Riley killing herself upon their reconciliation after years of estrangement. But Sasha senses an opportunity and assumes Riley's identity so she can escape her old life.

Playing Riley isn't without complications, though. Riley's had a strained relationship with her wife and stepson so Sasha must do whatever she can to make her newfound family love and accept her. If Sasha's arrangement ends, then she'll have nothing protecting her from her past. However, when one of Sasha's former clients tracks her down, Sasha must choose between her new life and the only person who cared about her.

But things are about to become even more complicated, as a third sister, Katrina, enters the scene...

The Ones That Got Away
By Lisa Hill

Have you ever had that feeling that you just needed to escape? Runaway from life, from all its problems; **be the one that got away?**

Tilly Henshaw has. Tilly wants to escape. Escape her suffocating mum, her dementing gran and finally shake off the stigmatism attached to ADHD; a condition she was diagnosed with when she was fourteen.

When the opportunity arises to escape to the sleepy, Cornish fishing village of Hope Cove, Tilly grabs it with both hands. But she soon discovers that she's not the only one who's runaway to Cornwall and everyone's keeping their reasons for escaping firmly to themselves.

As Tilly starts uncovering family secrets, she begins to understand there is no running away from your problems; you can't build a hopeful future without confronting who and what hurt you in your past.

Sirkkusaga
By Kyt Wright

A saga – a long story of heroic achievement, especially a medieval prose narrative in Old Norse or a long, involved story, account, or series of incidents often named for the principal character.

Several hundred years after an world-shattering war, two of the surviving nations, the Reignweald and the Dominion have fought themselves to a standstill, both remaining determined to control of what's left of it.

Sirki Vigsdottir, a songstress who performs under the name Freya in folk-rock group *The Harvest* is beautiful, self-centered woman who is fond of drink and a recovering addict to boot, not the sort of girl a boy brings home to mother.

Following an attack from an unexpected quarter, abilities awaken within Sirki, who begins a journey of self-discovery. These new found skills attract the attention of both the Psi, a mysterious group of telepaths headed by the fearsome Mina and an equally sinister government department; the ACG.

Sirki, learning the real truth of her origin, is dragged into plotting between the queen and the Government, finding herself in constant danger as Bren, fighting for the nation, becomes an important part of her life.As it becomes clear that her life of self-indulgence is over, Sirki wonders if her new-found powers are a blessing or a curse.

Arthur: Shadow of a God
By Richard Denham

King Arthur has fascinated the Western world for over a thousand years and yet we still know nothing more about him now than we did then. Layer upon layer of heroics and exploits has been piled upon him to the point where history, legend and myth have become hopelessly entangled.

In recent years, there has been a sort of scholarly consensus that 'the once and future king' was clearly some sort of Romano-British warlord, heroically stemming the tide of wave after wave of Saxon invaders after the end of Roman rule. But surprisingly, and no matter how much we enjoy this narrative, there is actually next-to-nothing solid to support this theory except the wishful thinking of understandably bitter contemporaries. The sources and scholarship used to support the 'real Arthur' are as much tentative guesswork and pushing 'evidence' to the extreme to fit in with this version as anything involving magic swords, wizards and dragons. Even Archaeology remains silent. Arthur is, and always has been, the square peg that refuses to fit neatly into the historians round hole.

Arthur: Shadow of a God gives a fascinating overview of Britain's lost hero and casts a light over an often-overlooked and somewhat inconvenient truth; Arthur was almost certainly not a man at all, but a god. He is linked inextricably to the world of Celtic folklore and Druidic traditions. Whereas tyrants like Nero and Caligula were men who fancied themselves gods; is it not possible that Arthur was a god we have turned into a man? Perhaps then there is a truth here. Arthur, 'The King under the Mountain'; sleeping until his return will never return, after all, because he doesn't need to. Arthur the god never left in the first place and remains as popular today as he ever was. His legend echoes in stories, films and games that are every bit as imaginative and fanciful as that which the minds of talented bards such as Taliesin and Aneirin came up with when the mists of the 'dark ages' still swirled over Britain – and perhaps that is a good thing after all, most at home in the imaginations of children and adults alike – being the Arthur his believers want him to be.

A Storm of Magic
By Ashley Laino

Being brought back from the dead is an impressive trick, even for magician Darien Burron. Now he must try and use his sleight of hand to swindle modern-day witch, Mirah, to sign her power away, or end up a tormented demon in the afterlife.

Meanwhile, sixteen-year-old Mirah is starting to lose control of her powers. After an incident at her aunt's Witchery store, Mirah is sent to a secret coven to learn to control her abilities. While away, Mirah meets up with a soft-spoken clairvoyant, a brazen storm witch, and the creator of dark magic itself. The young woman must learn to trust in herself before she loses herself entirely to the darkness that hunts her.

Weirder War Two
By Richard Denham & Michael Jecks

Did a Warner Bros. cartoon prophesize the use of the atom bomb? Did the Allies really plan to use stink bombs on the enemy? Why did the Nazis make their own version of Titanic and why were polar bear photographs appearing throughout Europe?

The Second World War was the bloodiest of all wars. Mass armies of men trudged, flew or rode from battlefields as far away as North Africa to central Europe, from India to Burma, from the Philippines to the borders of Japan. It saw the first aircraft carrier sea battle, and the indiscriminate use of terror against civilian populations in ways not seen since the Thirty Years War. Nuclear and incendiary bombs erased entire cities. V weapons brought new horror from the skies: the V1 with their hideous grumbling engines, the V2 with sudden, unexpected death. People were systematically starved: in Britain food had to be rationed because of the stranglehold of U-Boats, while in Holland the German blockage of food and fuel saw 30,000 die of starvation in the winter of 1944/5. It was a catastrophe for millions.

At a time of such enormous crisis, scientists sought ever more inventive weapons, or devices to help halt the war. Civilians were involved as never before, with women taking up new trades, proving themselves as capable as their male predecessors whether in the factories or the fields.

The stories in this book are of courage, of ingenuity, of hilarity in some cases, or of great sadness, but they are all thought-provoking - and rather weird. So whether you are interested in the last Polish cavalry charge, the Blackout Ripper, Dada, or Ghandi's attempt to stop the bloodshed, welcome to the Weirder War Two!

**Click Bait
By Gillian Philip**

A funny joke's a funny joke. Eddie Doolan doesn't think twice about adapting it to fit a tragic local news story and posting it on social media.

It's less of a joke when his drunken post goes viral. It stops being funny altogether when Eddie ends up jobless, friendless and ostracized by the whole town of Langburn. This isn't how he wanted to achieve fame.

Under siege from the press, and facing charges not just for the joke but for a history of abusive behavior on the internet, Eddie grows increasingly paranoid and desperate. The only people still speaking to him are Crow, a neglected kid who relies on Eddie for food and company, and Sid, the local gamekeeper's granddaughter. It's Sid who offers Eddie a refuge and an understanding ear.

But she also offers him an illegal shotgun - and as Eddie's life spirals downwards, and his efforts at redemption are thwarted at every turn, the gun starts to look like the answer to all his problems.

**Father of Storms
By Dean Jones**

Imagine losing everything you loved as well as the future you'd wished for so long to come true.

Seth was born with the gift to manipulate energy, unfortunately his skills mark him as a target for one who wishes to control everything. So began a life running from those who would seek to command him, a life that spans over a thousand years waiting for the day when all will be once again as it was.

Captured in modern day London, Seth needs the help of his companions, the Mara, to show him who he is through dreams of his past, so he can save the family he has waited so long to have. A warrior bred for battle must fight once more but this time the battlefield is his mind. Can Seth win, or will he finally lose who he is and become the weapon of the man who started his nightmare all those years ago? *Father of Storms* is a story told through time, a tale of love and hope where there seems to be none and above all it is a reminder that if you believe, truly believe then even from the darkest places, good things come to those who wait.

www.blkdogpublishing.com